Table of Contents

"Words have no power to impress the mind without the exquisite horror of their reality."

~Edgar Allan Poe

Photo by D. Pardee Whiting / PardeeTime Photos - 2016

"Writing is the painting of the voice" ~Voltaire

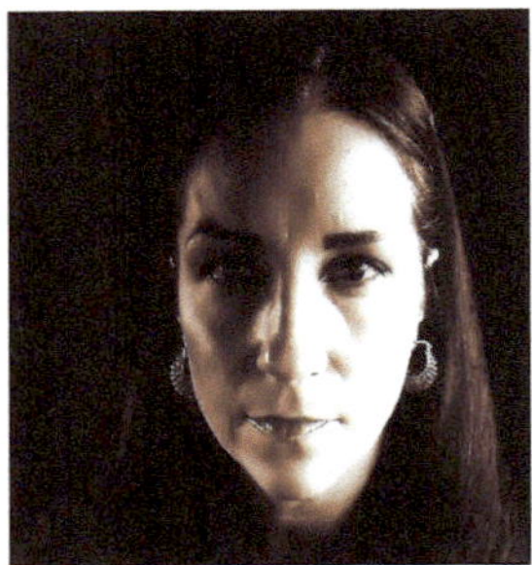

Lisa Vasquez holds the record for most hobbies acquired during the 2020 Pandemic while juggling the House of Stitched, and her Unsaintly household. When she's not drawing, planting, writing, painting, and cooking, she's forgetting where here glasses are (on her face) and reheating her cup of coffee for the third time. You can find her menagerie of madness on UNSAINTLY.WIKI or on Instagram @ Unsaintly

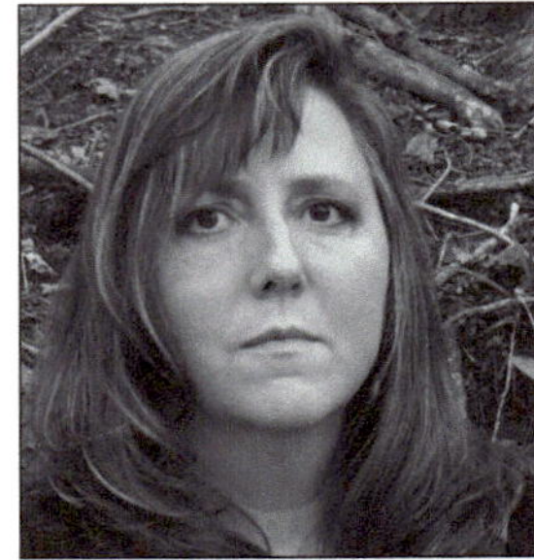

Donelle Pardee Whiting keeps her muse in the form of a dragon that often suffers from squirrel syndrome, and she shares her home with her husband and their two dogs, Clara Dogswald the Wonder Husky and Polly Esther the Not a Husky. She raised one son who has five littles of his own. At some point the squirrels will let her go live with a website, but until then you can follow her Instagram @ dwhiting_pardeetime.

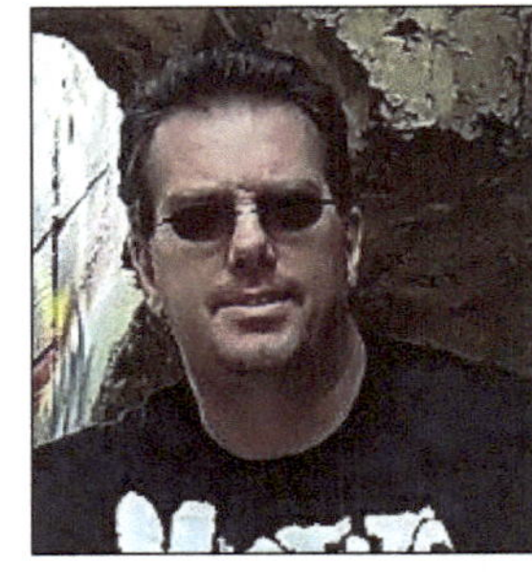

A.J. Brown is a southern-born writer who tells emotionally charged, character driven stories that often delve into the dark parts of the human psyche. Though he writes mostly darker stories, he does so without unnecessary gore, coarse language, or sex. More than 200 of his stories have been published in various online and print publications.

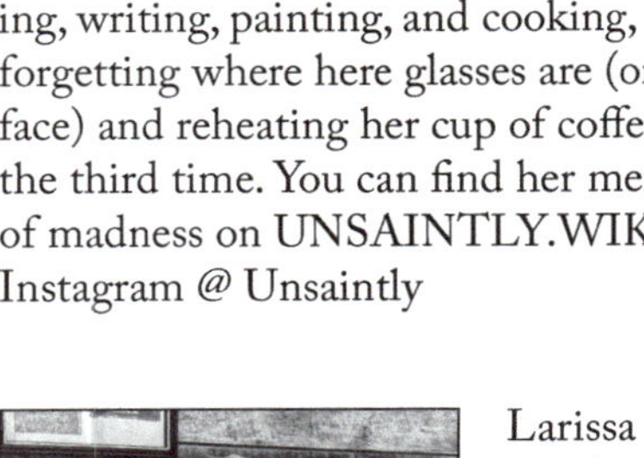

Larissa Bennett lives in Western New York with her wife and their four fur babies. She has a love of poetry and horror, as well as mystery, fantasy, and mythological creatures. When not writing, she enjoys spending time with her family, gardening on their farm in Western New York, doing crochet, hiking, reading, and creating faerie gardens. Aside from working with Stitched Smile Publications, she works with individuals with developmental disabilities and also does freelance editing.

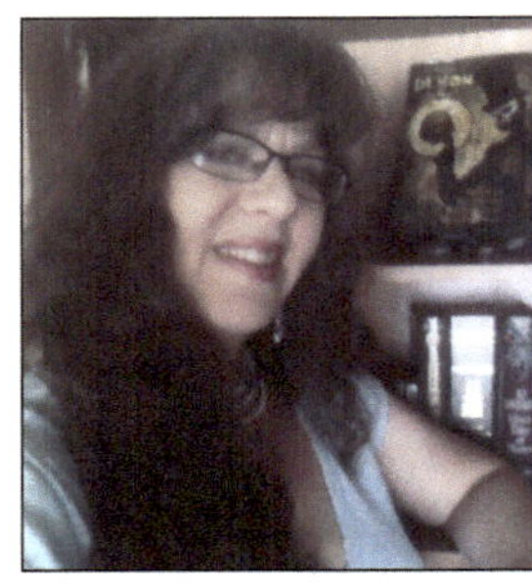

Lisa Lee is a freelance editor and runs the review blog *Bibliophilia Templum*. She received her first book for her fourth birthday, which her oldest sister taught her to read within a week. Now an avid reader, Lisa maintains a home library arranged by genre and alphabetized by author.

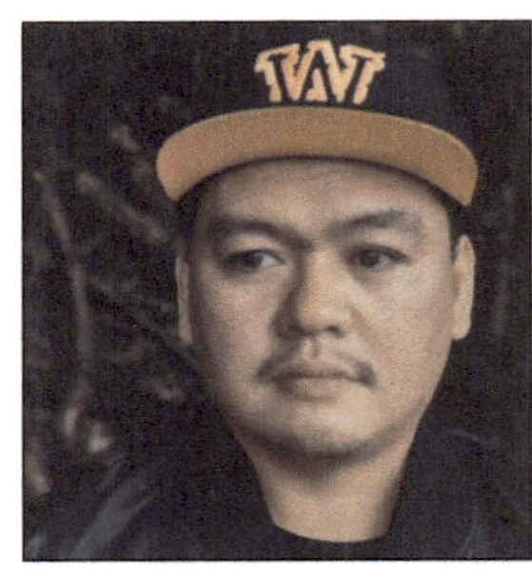

Aurelio Rico Lopez III hails from Iloilo City, Philippines. A self-diagnosed scribble junkie and horror enthusiast, he has authored a variety of works of poetry and fiction, including *Two Drinks Away From Chaos*, *Kaiju Double Barrel*, *Not the Forgiving Kind*, and *Hangover of the Apocalypse*. You may find and reach Aurelio on Facebook or email him at thirdylopez2001@yahoo.com.

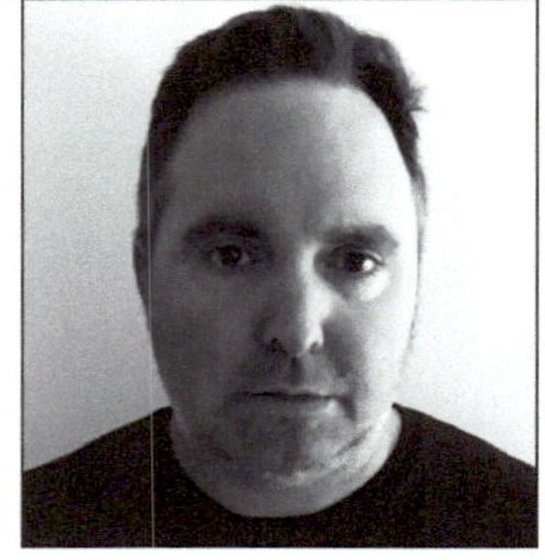

Peter Molnar is the author of *Broken Birds* and the forthcoming novella collection "*Rhapsody in Red*. He has been a singer/songwriter and an author of literary horror for three decades. He lives and works in Southeastern Pennsylvania.

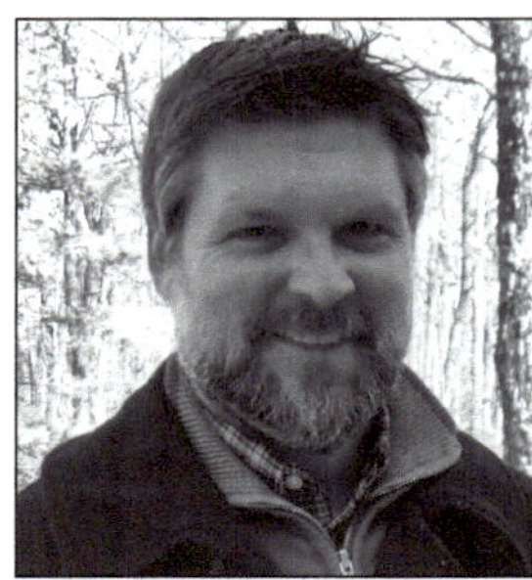

Ezekiel Kincaid was a pastor for twenty years and uses his experiences with the supernatural and human condition to influence his horror stories. He also has a sarcastic side and enjoys writing comedic horror. He will fight anyone who says they don't like Bruce Campbell.

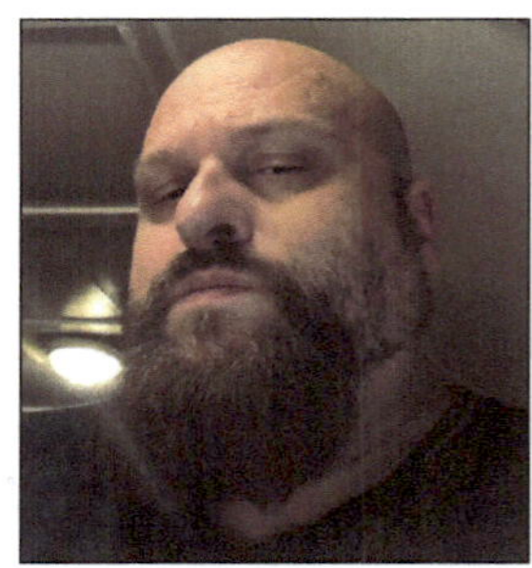

Thomas R. Clark is a musician, writer, and podcast producer and engineer. He is the author of *Bella's Boys* and *Good Boy*, published through Stitched Smile Publications. Tom lives in Central New York with his wife and a trio of Jack Russell Terrier companions.

A letter to the reader ...

Writing a letter to an anonymous reader is sometimes like writing in a diary. I'm the only person I know for sure is reading it. My hope is for this not to be true with the magazine you are about to immerse yourself within. "There's a story in everything," Jeff said to me. In fact, he made it his catchphrase. Indulge me a moment, and I'll tell you the story behind the magazine.

In 2016, when I first began Stitched Smile Publications, I really wanted it to be a full-service company. I envisioned myself kicking in the doors of the industry and making a change to how the world saw independent authors. In 2018, we attempted this magazine one time and realized how much more work goes into the production. Needless to say, it wasn't everything *we* hoped it would be. As a group, we took a step back and went back to the drawing board. There was a long wait, pieces on the chess board were moved around, and then ... 2020 happened.

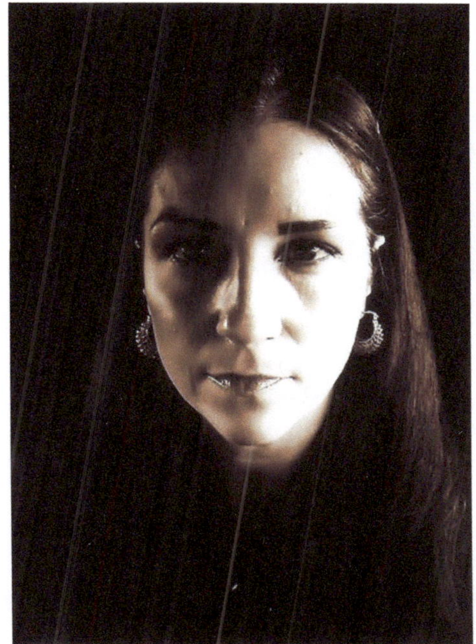

Let's face it; 2020 is the monster we all wish was fiction. Unfortunately, it's real and it's what's on everyone's plate. For us at the House of Stitched, it was a big, slimy, pile of crap with moldy cheese and rotten tomatoes. Between staff getting ill, authors getting ill, and the world being shut away, we decided to head into the "dragon den" and hibernate until we could come back at full strength.

I want to thank Donelle for stepping up and taking the reigns on this project. Between us, the shared love and desire for this to become a reality has left us itching to get started. We knew it had to wait, but it wasn't easy. I also want to thank my staff for believing in us, even though we've tripped and stumbled along the way. The loyalty of everyone who has stood by the House of Stitched name is humbling and something to be talked about. You guys will never go without hearing your praises.

As we always do, we adapted. This is the new face, and we are proud to show it to you. We hope you enjoy the pages within which are filled with the "stories from everything." Our hope is to bring you into the experience of storytelling, the process of the writer's mind, and be a beacon in the world of dark fiction.

We hope all of you are safe and are surviving as best you can in a world full of changes and uncertainty.

Keep turning the page,

Lisa Vasquez
CEO Stitched Smile Publications

From the editor's desk

Welcome to House of Stitched.

Stitched Smile Publications' very own magazine.

Do come in. Take your shoes off. Make yourselves at home and sit a spell. I'll be your host along with Lisa Vasquez. You know Lisa. She is the Unsaintly Queen, the CEO of SSP who wholeheartedly supported and, of course helped a great deal, with this publication.

Before we go any further, I also do need to offer immense gratitude and appreciation to everyone who contributed content, to those who patiently answered my questions, and best friends and family who talked me back from the ledge when I got too close. You are all

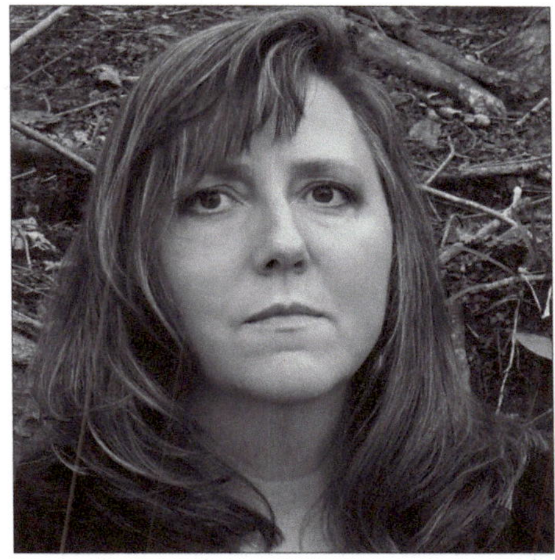

valued.

And who am I? Aside from being your guide along your journey through our pages, I am a writer, a journalist—the good kind, an editor, a photographer. What will you find locked inside the House that Stitched built? You will see artwork, photos, a little bit of trivia, original fiction, and of course feature articles about people and events you know—or want to know. A lot of time and work went into this inaugural edition, and all of us at SSP plan to bring you future issues with more original content. So, be sure to come back time and time again.

Now that we are all comfortable, and the formalities are done, we can settle in and explore the place we call "home." So, grab a beverage and snack of your choosing, and lose yourself in our world for a bit.

And as always ...

I will see you on the next page.

Donelle Pardee Whiting

Managing Editor

The Write Way
with A.J. Brown

Plaguing Your Mind?

I have a habit of being blunt when it comes to writing. I tend to see things a bit differently and some folks, shall we say, aren't fans of my opinions. That's okay. I'll be fine, and so will they.

That brings me to a point I want to make, one I feel is a must for writers (and anyone who does anything in life). Recently, in a Facebook group for writers, a question was asked, which at first I wasn't certain was sincere. After I read it a second, then a third time, I didn't care if it was sincere; I was annoyed the question was even asked. The question is as follows (minus the name of the guilty party):

"I have a question that has been plaguing my mind lately. Is it better to put a lot of time and energy into making a project good, or to not care about quality and just get it done and out there to make a fast dime, because the readers don't know nor care?"

Read it again. I'll wait. Pretend the *Jeopardy* song is playing.

…

…

Okay, did you get that? Did your head just explode? There are three issues with this question, and I will address them in order.

I have a question that has been plaguing my mind lately.

This struck me as serious, and I immediately stopped and said, "Hold on, Brownie. Let's see what is plaguing this poor guy." It's a great way to get someone's attention, and it certainly got mine. The actual question sent me down YouGotta-BeKiddingMe Boulevard. The first part of that question was:

Is it better to put a lot of time and energy into making a project good, or to not care about quality and just get it done and out there to make a fast dime …

If this is the question that is really bothering you to the point of plaguing your mind, then you probably shouldn't be looking to publish a book, or do anything artistic or that you get paid money for. This reeks of laziness.

Every response was similar: quality, quality, quality.

My response was no different, but I added a little more to it. Why, as any artist, would you want to put out something subpar just to make a few bucks? You have to put your name on the story. You have to stand behind that story and say, "You'll love it," and portray that the book is your best effort.

As writers, if you set out to make money in this business, then you had best write a great story, and you most certainly need to put care, time, and energy into making the project, not just good, but great.

If you are going to do it, do it right or don't do it at all.

As if the first part of that question wasn't bad enough, the second part is what riled me up.

… because the readers don't know nor care …

This bothers me more than everything else. Here's the thing, a truth I feel everyone who writes a story with the intention to publish should understand: if you don't put the effort and care into your work to make it as good as it can be, the reader *will* know, and they *will* care. Readers can spot when something is done with a lazy pen (or fingers, as it may be). They will be disgusted they wasted their money, and more importantly, their time reading your lazy work. When a reader feels like a writer didn't try or didn't put enough effort into a story to make it as good as it can be they will spread the word to all of their friends, and it will not be pretty.

"Don't purchase that book by Writer McWritesbad. It's not good, and it's poorly written."

That is putting it nicely.

As a writer seeking publication, it is your responsibility to take your readers into consideration. Is the book you just sloppily wrote something *you* would want to purchase and read? Is it something you would be fine with being on your shelf? Is it something you would say great things about to other potential readers? As a writer, is this something you would stand behind and say, "I did my best." If you can say no to any of those questions, you're doing it wrong.

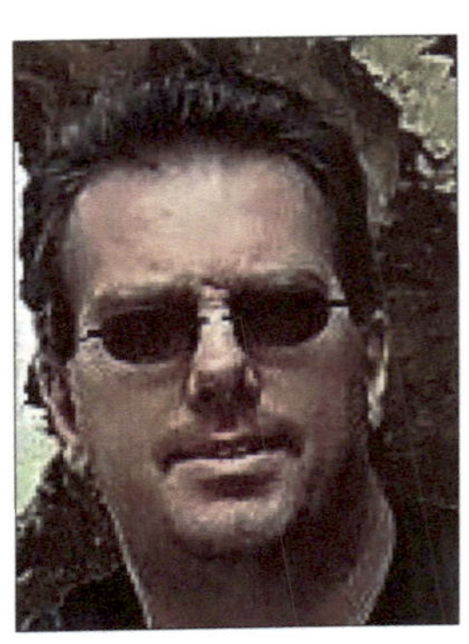

By stating the readers don't know and don't care, this writer has completely disrespected and disregarded the people he relies on to purchase his book, leave him good reviews, and spread the word about him and his stories. He has said, "Screw the reader, they don't matter to me." It's the ultimate "What they don't know, won't hurt them." You won't have many readers and even less fans if this is your mindset.

With everything you do, especially something that is an expression of art as writing is, you should want it to shine. You should want it to be its best because you love what you do and what you create. You shouldn't slap it together because you want to make a "dime." If you do, a dime is probably all you will make.

Here's a question for you: Is it more important for you to make a dime or three or to put out a quality piece of work that could lead to greater things, bigger audiences,

See WRITE, page 9

"Behold with attention this place of terror where the vanities of this world of illusions are over."

Words found on a plaque above the cemetery outside of town in Castelo Rodrigo

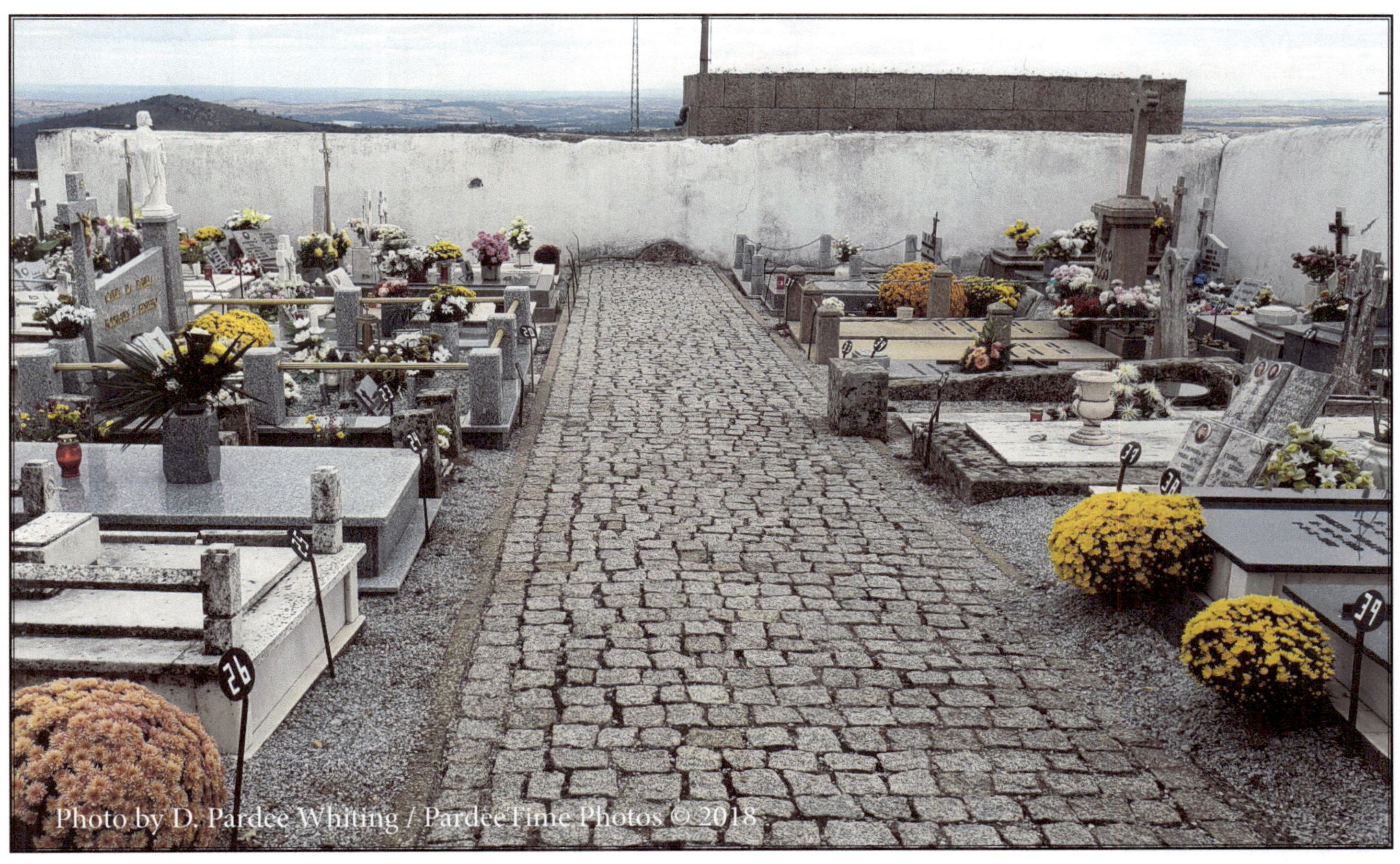

Photo by D. Pardee Whiting / PardeeTime Photos © 2018

Become One with Your Story

By Ezekiel Kincaid

Writing is more than mastering the English language. It is learning how to become "one" with your characters and setting. Don't get me wrong; knowing the rules of grammar makes for smooth reading, but if your words don't bleed you end up with a bland, dry story.

What do I mean by become "one" with your story?

Writing for me is a meditation exercise. Once I have the gist of my story and my characters, I sit down at my computer, close my eyes, and clear my mind. I then try and become one with my character. I get inside their head, their heart, their soul, and their emotions. Why are they feeling the way they are in this moment? What has happened in their life to shape them and make them who they are? What are their joys and sorrows? Their pains and regrets? What was their upbringing, and where are they from? What are their mannerisms?

After I have entered the soul of my character I then focus on their surroundings. I take in what their five senses are picking up. What do they see? What are the smells around them? What do they hear? Are they touching something or holding something in their hand? Are they drinking or eating, or is their mouth dry from fear? In other words, after becoming one with my character I then seek to become one with their surroundings.

I then begin to see the world through my character's eyes. As the story progresses, I take personally what happens to my characters. This allows me to insert real, raw emotions into the tale. Sometimes it is like watching a movie play in my mind. I see with vividness everything happening. This also helps with describing the right amount of detail for the reader so they can picture what is taking place.

The next thing I do is insert a piece of myself into the character and story. I conjure up the emotions and experiences in my own life that have shaped me. This helps me to form a deeper bond with my character. I have had hard times. I have had sorrows and joys; grief and gain; heartache and happiness. Every time I do this it is like taking a knife to an old wound and cutting it open again. This is what allows me to bleed into my characters and stories.

As writers we cannot be afraid to take the things which have shaped us, no matter how painful or joyful, and pour those things into our stories. This is what separates a good writer from a great writer. Great writers are not afraid to slit the wrist of their souls, hold them over the page, and let the life drain from them and seep into the page.

The other thing we must do if we are going to write in this manner is to take in our surroundings. Learn to be an observant person. Watch the people around you and take note of their speech and mannerisms. Notice the sights, sounds, and smells as you go about your daily life. Make mental notes of these things, and when you sit down to write, recall them.

I get asked to review books all the time, and I have to pass on nine out of ten of them. Why? Sometimes it is because they are poorly written. Other times it is because the tale falls flat and is void of what makes us human or full of one dimensional, unrelatable characters.

My encouragement to writers, both new and seasoned, is to yes get a firm grasp on the English language. But even more so, bleed into your work. Can this be exhausting and draining? You better believe it. Every time I finish a writing session I am spent.

So, you need to ask yourself if you are willing to pay the price and make the sacrifice. Are you content with being a good writer or do you want to write in a way that sets you apart from all the other clamoring voices out there? Only you can answer this question for yourself.

I already know what my answer is.

Rachel's Circle

I've learned not to question when the dead come to me. Now, I welcome them and listen to their tales. One such visitor was a young girl named Rachel. She wouldn't tell me her last name, but she did tell me what happened to her.

"Mr. Kincaid."

I was taken out of my world of writing by a young, sweet voice.

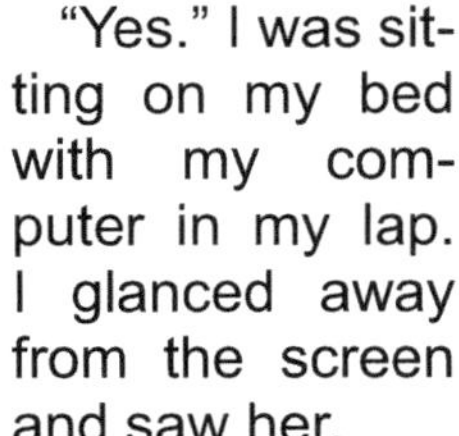

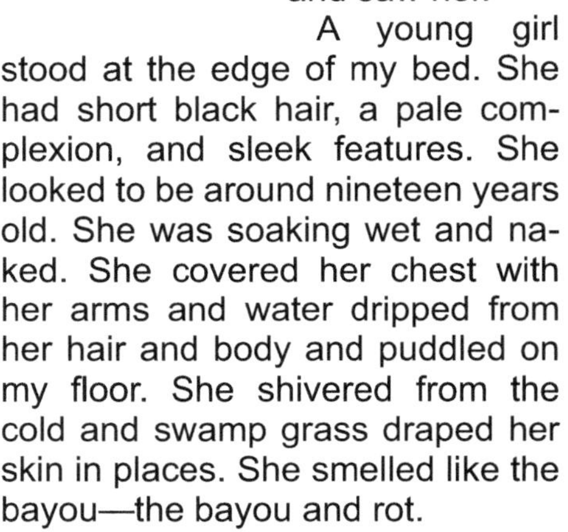

"Yes." I was sitting on my bed with my computer in my lap. I glanced away from the screen and saw her.

A young girl stood at the edge of my bed. She had short black hair, a pale complexion, and sleek features. She looked to be around nineteen years old. She was soaking wet and naked. She covered her chest with her arms and water dripped from her hair and body and puddled on my floor. She shivered from the cold and swamp grass draped her skin in places. She smelled like the bayou—the bayou and rot.

"I'm cold," she said, her teeth chattering.

I studied the girl. Her lips were cracked and purple. "Come on," I said and motioned with my head. I pulled back the blanket.

The girl crawled in and covered herself. She curled up in a ball next to me and stared up with green, solemn eyes.

"My name's Rachel," she said then swallowed. Her throat made a crackling sound. "And I need your help."

"Why?"

"I'm alone and afraid here." Rachel sat up in the bed and wrapped the covers around her. "I—I guess I should tell you what happened. Or, show you rather." Rachel held out her hand to me, palm upwards.

I lifted my hand from the keyboard in a slow, steady motion and placed it in hers. Rachel's skin was cold, wet, and clammy. I closed my eyes and was taken deep into a Louisiana swamp. I saw Rachel kneeling in the middle of a protective circle she had drawn around herself with the knife in her hand. Her voice narrated.

"I was being groomed to be a blood thorn witch. I was accepted into a coven and was taught the old and ancient ways."

Her naked body swayed, and a gentle breeze rippled her hair.

"I had already sliced my hand and given my blood to the keepers of the forest world. I had studied Grimoire and thought I could handle it."

An owl screeched and landed on a branch above Rachel.

"A presence appeared in the circle. It was dark and menacing. It gave a low growl.

I saw an entity standing in the circle with Rachel. I had seen him and dealt with him many times before. He was tall and skinny with red hair and pointy features. He wore a black suit and sunglasses. He was a Leviathan demon and he goes by the name "The Philistine."

"I gave myself to the god and goddess."

I knew who they were. This god and goddess were Leviathan and Lilith.

"The old ways either lead to madness, death, or a great poetic spirit. I think you can guess what happened to me. I realized in those moments the circle of protection doesn't work when you've already invited it in."

I saw Rachel take the blade of the knife and slice both her arms from wrist to forearm. The copper scent of her warm blood filled the forest, and she toppled to the ground. The Philistine stood over her then he turned and saw me.

His features contorted, and he

See ONE, page 9

Gothic Betty Crocker Presents ...

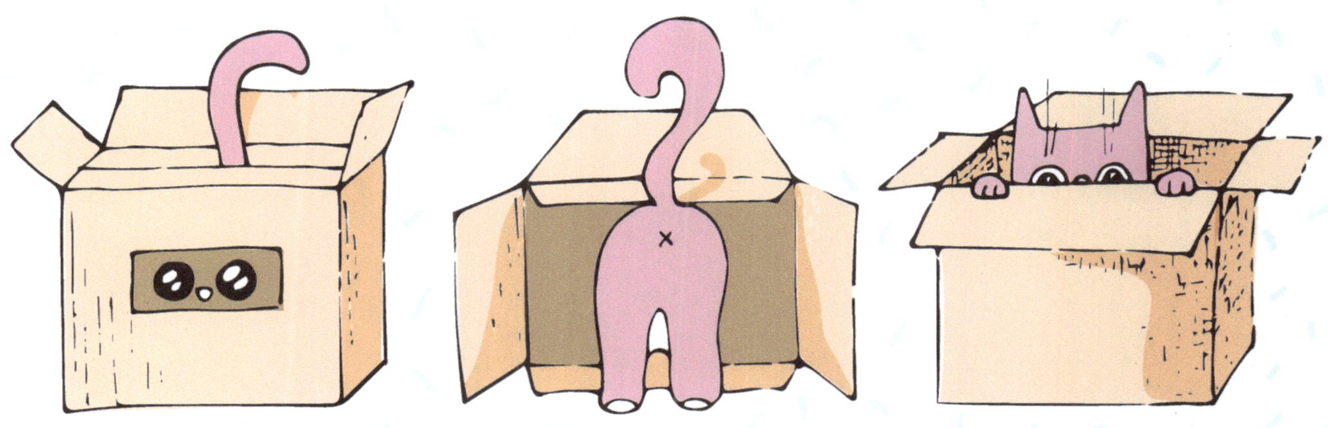

Kitty Litter Cake

I don't remember where I got the original recipe for this, but I remember the looks on those beautiful, innocent faces sitting around the table to sing "Happy Birthday" to my youngest son who just turned 8.

Don't miss an opportunity to record them yourself when you put this on the table.

What you'll need:

1 package chocolate cake mix
1 package white cake mix
2 packages instant vanilla pudding mix
1 package vanilla sandwich cookies
3 drops green food coloring
1 package tootsie rolls
1 NEW Kitty Litter Pan
1 NEW Kitty Pooper Scooper

I prefer to use a food processor but you can do this all by hand if you like.

Directions

Step 1
Prepare cake mixes and bake according to package directions (any size pan).

Step 2
Prepare pudding according to package directions and chill until ready to assemble.

Step 3
Crumble sandwich cookies in small batches in a food processor. Eat one cookie to be sure it's not really kitty litter *wink wink*

Set aside entire mix minus 1/4 cup. In the 1/4 cup you've set aside, add a few drops of green food coloring and mix well.

Step 4
Once the cakes are cooled to room temperature, use your hands or a fork to crumble them into a large bowl. Mix this with 1/2 of the remaining cookie crumbs, and the chilled pudding. Use only enough pudding to help the mix to stick together. You don't want the litter to look soggy and peed in. No one will eat that.

Step 5
Take CLEAN kitty litter box (please don't use Fluffy's) and line it with kitty liner or parchment paper, then pour cake mixture into box.

Step 6
Unwrap and line a microwave safe dish with your toostie rolls and heat until softened. Times may vary so watch them carefully. You don't want mushy piles that look like Fluffy got into the trash again. Here's the best part. You want to use your fingers to shape the "turds." You can hang some off the edge and even bury some (which is hilarious when you watch the faces of those you're about to serve.) Make sure you roll a few of them in the green/white "litter" for authenticity. Remember! This is an ART.

Step 7
Set up your camera and serve with the pooper scooper to your unsuspecting vict—I mean, guests.

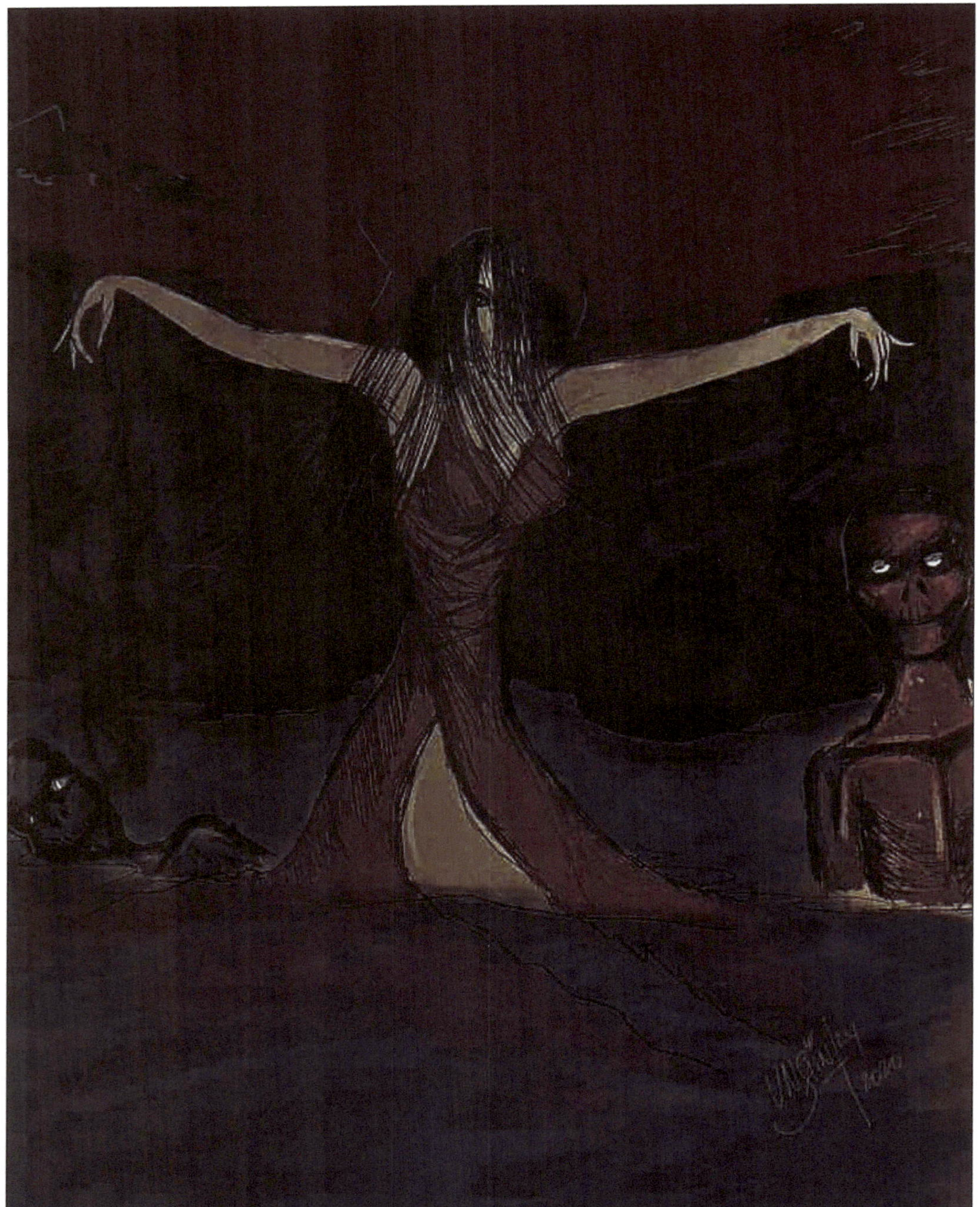

Lady Death

She is pestilence

Walking the Earth bringing death

Souls are hers to take

Artwork by Lisa Vasquez

https://unsaintly.wiki/artist

https://unsaintlyart.wordpress.com

https://www.facebook.com/groups/unsaintlyart

On Instagram @unsaintly

Haiku by D. Pardee Whiting

On Twitter @pardeetime

On Instagram @dwhiting_pardeetime

https://www.facebook.com/pardee-whiting

ONE, cont. from page 7

grew angry. "You can't help her," he said. "I got to her first." He smirked then scooped Rachel's body up and walked towards the swamp.

Rachel let go of my hand, and I opened my eyes. She stared deep into me.

"I couldn't find the light of God in life. Can you help me find it in death?" Rachel gazed at me with a face pleading for hope.

I reached and grabbed my Bible off the floor and opened it to "John, Chapter 1." I read to her. "In the beginning was the Word, and the Word was with God, and the Word was God. He was in the beginning with God. All things were made through him, and without him was not anything made. In him was life, and this life was the light of me. The light shines in the darkness, and the darkness has not overcome it."

"Thank you," Rachel smiled. She held out her arms, showed me her scars, then faded away.

To him who is in fear everything rustles
~Sophacles

WRITE, cont. from page 5

and potentially, more than a dime? Think about it. If you answered money over quality, yeah, you're in the wrong business.

Period. I'm done here. Mic drop. Lower the curtain.

A.J.

LIBER AUTOPSIA

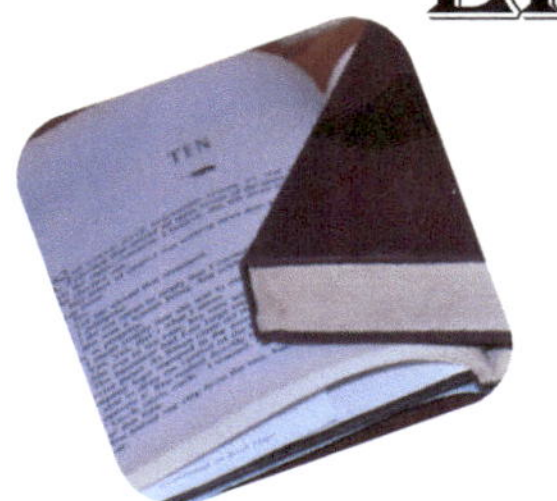

with

Lisa Lee

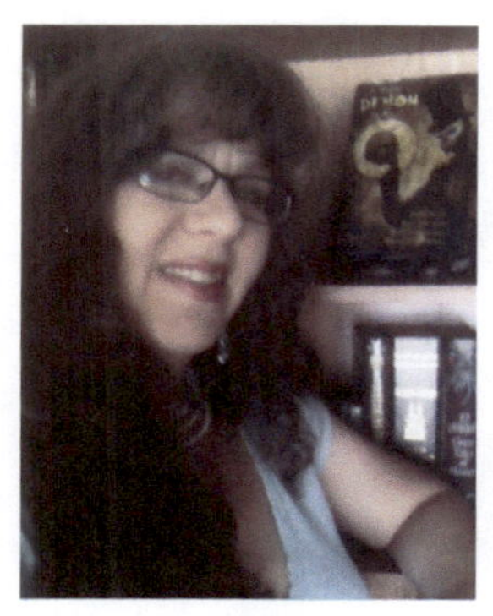

Kelli Owen combines relevance with entertainment

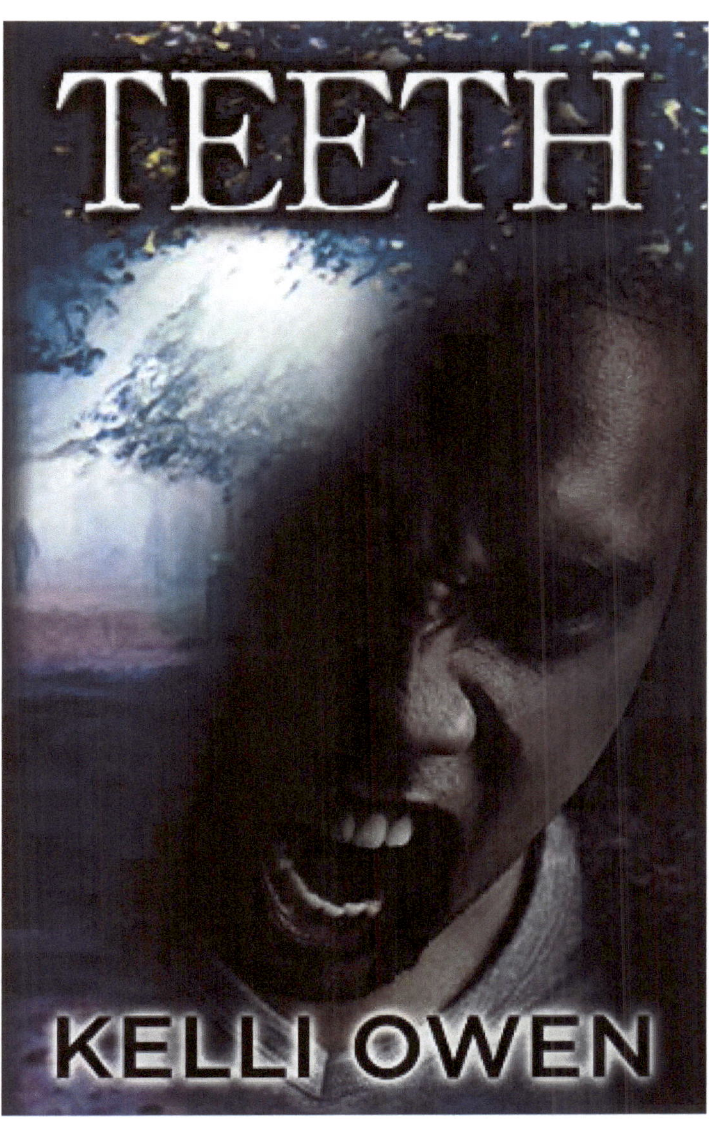

Teeth
Kelli Owen

Print Length: 250 pages
Published by Gypsy Press (August 3, 2018)

Synopsis:

All myths have a kernel of truth. The truth is: vampires are real. They've always been here but only came out of hiding in the last century. They are not what Hollywood would have you believe. They are not what is written in lore or whispered by the superstitious. They look and act like humans. They live and love and die like humans. Puberty is just a bit more stressful for those with the recessive gene. And while some teenagers worry about high school, others dread their next set of teeth. Vampires are real, but in a social climate still struggling to accept that truth, do teeth alone make them monsters?

Review:

Teeth by Kelli Owen is a masterwork addition to the horror subgenre of vampirism. The story is woven from two interconnected plots that illustrate timelessly relevant sociological and psychological issues and horrors. Owen's expert characterization and storytelling will enthrall you as her story bleeds your heart and mind.Before I continue, I feel the need to point out, with all due respect to other reviewers, bigotry and prejudice are NOT the only issues this novel illustrates. I don't want readers to avoid this story thinking it is one big political statement. Nor do I want readers to only see that when they read it. There is much more to this story than the plight of both historic and modern societies. This story is about cause and effect, self-loathing and self-acceptance, fear and love, bullying and sacrifice, mental illness, and misinformation. This is a big picture story told by a literary black belt. And, as with all great works, it can be enjoyed purely for entertainment value if you choose to tune out the sociological relevance. The story stands on its merit both as a relevant literary piece and as an entertaining read.To continue, Owen's expert characterization is, in my opinion, a vital part of her

See TEETH, page 12

Scream

By Larissa Bennett

And I, being small and insignificant,
Scream silently into the barren night.
A wolf howls in the distance—did it hear me?
Did it hear my cries—is it possible?

I'm screaming—to find the words,
To release all that is locked inside me.
I'm screaming—to break free from this cage,
It has become my existence.

I'm screaming to escape this bitter solitude;
At the rage of a lone life—void of the connection
That grounds me to who I am.
I'm screaming from the fear
I will be left within the chasm of my mind.
I'm screaming from the pain I feel,
From losing those whom I loved—
Those who have left me behind.

I'm screaming at you to open your eyes,
See who is standing before you.
I'm screaming to break out,
To have the strength to become who I want to be.
I'm screaming so the tears I hold in
Will not spill out of my soul.

I'm screaming for you—for me—can't you hear?

Through my screams the wolf continues to howl,
Its lone voice echoing through the stillness.
I wonder, is it grieving?
I run towards the sound, desperate to know—
Could this wolf feel as I do?
The air is thick and filled with dust.

Each breath is heavy—the wind cools as the rain falls.
Slow at first, then torrents that shield the mountain.
The ground becomes slick beneath me.
Lightning streaks the sky in lines of blinding white,
Thunder shakes the earth—the air trembles.
The thunder echoes through the valley.
Lightning strikes the ground—
Tall-standing trees ignite into flames.

The storm passes over the land,
A path of destruction in its wake.
I am in the middle of it.

All around, trees are uprooted,
Blown down from the ferocity of the wind.
Blackened trees lay scattered in an empty field,
Lightning burned away the life that was once inside.

The storm has passed, and I am left
Drenched in a tangle of mutilated death.
Silence surrounds me as the wind and rain move on.
I cry out to the wolf—its sorrowful howl replies.
I run towards the sound; it fills me as I draw closer.

He is surrounded by the burning corpses of trees,
Their charred bodies smoldering.
We stand in the darkness together, surveying the damage.
I fall to the ground as despair washes over me.

I gaze into the eyes of the wolf and grieve.
I grieve for what we have lost.
All hope seems lost for our two souls.

I scream into the barren night, at the brutality and the beauty.
We scream together at the toil we face.
We scream so we won't give up.

Sarcophagus

By Aurelio Lopez III

Navigating blindly
inside unchartered
maze of tunnels,
each stretch and corner
identical to the last.

Might as well be
running in circles.

Nevertheless,
pulse racing and
adrenaline pumping,
he continues his flight,
splashing through
filthy puddles and
breathing the foul air.

The batteries in
his flashlight
have long run out,
yet he dares not discard
the torch.

Finally, he slams against
an impenetrable barrier.
His fingers search
desperately for a latch,
a door, a secret entry
but finds none.

He turns, back to the wall
to face the darkness.
In the gloom,
the unmistakable stench
of death, heralded by
the scuttling sound
of a thousand insects.

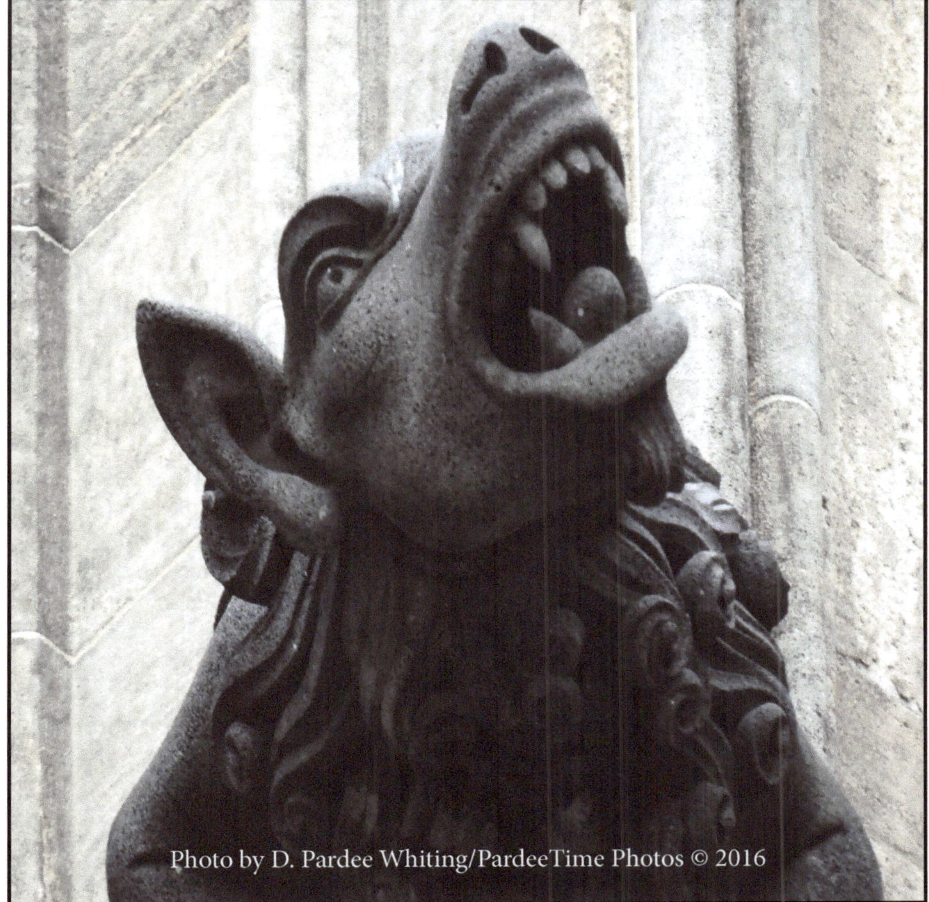

Photo by D. Pardee Whiting/PardeeTime Photos © 2016

TEETH, cont. from page 10

expert storytelling. The characters in *Teeth* are representative of real people and types of people without being the expected stereotypes. They have individual personalities and just enough backstory to keep their words and actions believable, if sometimes infuriating. They are clearly products of their life experiences, as real people are. And Kelli Owen does this without overwriting, which is why I say she is expert level. In addition to *Teeth* being a profound literary mirror of sociological plight with incredibly engaging characters, it is a good story. It is a compelling and fun read. Owen seems to have collected different ancient lore of a similar bent and melded them into a singular historic theme. It's brilliant and brilliantly done. To be clear, this is a horror novel. It has disturbing and horrifying sequences and subject matter. It does not fall under urban fantasy vampires even though it deviates from the Nosferatu style of vampirism. This unique piece is wholly Kelli Owen and completely shelf-worthy for the discerning reader.

Read it because it is a vampire horror novel.

Read it because it is impactful and socially relevant.

Read it because it is a good story. Read it because Kelli Owen wrote it.

Read it.

Everything becomes magnified at night. Sound travels in a different way, it's dark, and everything seems far more spooky.
~ Jo Brand

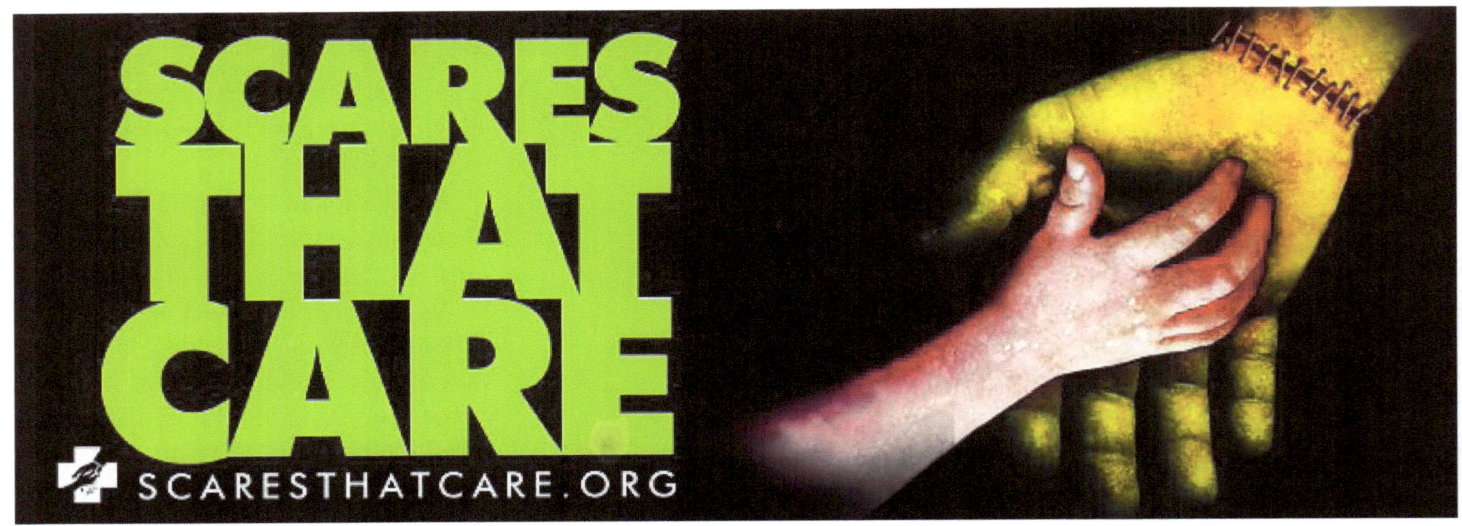

Horror fans gather to fight real monsters, help families

THE RIPPLE EFFECT

By D. Pardee Whiting

With so many non-profit charities in existence these days, it can be difficult to choose which one to support; however, horror fans discovered one in the form of Scares That Care, founded by Joe Ripple in 1996 as a tribute to a friend's daughter who had become terminally ill.

"Back when I was [police] detective, my partner had a daughter who contracted an inoperable brain tumor and passed when she was four," Ripple explained. "I had the honor to be one of her pallbearers at her funeral, and I saw how it really impacted the family."

This impact was not only financial but mental, as well. Because there are so many factors involved in the loss of a loved one, Ripple wanted to be able to do something. Not just for his police partner, but for anyone who needs help.

At the time his partner's daughter got sick, Ripple also worked as the head of security at HorrorFind, a major East Coast horror convention. He started doing research and discovered the horror community as a whole did not have their own banner with which to give back to the community.

"So I put two and two together, and Scares That Care was born," he said.

When asked why he chose the horror community and the name Scares That Care, Ripple explained it all started at the HorrorFind convention. As head of security at such an event, he was tasked with going in and potentially dealing with people who are doing cosplay, dressing up as Michael Myers, Jason Voorhees, Leatherface, and characters like that.

He started to wonder "Okay, how am I going to deal with these types of situations? If there's a fight. If there's a problem. If there's an incident. How am I going to deal with it?"

As security, Ripple's job was to see to the safety of the attendees, celebrities, and of the organization as a whole; it made him sad to think it could be a major issue or a major problem to deal with, he said, adding it turned out to be a non-issue.

"I'll give you an example. The first time I went into HorrorFind as head of security, there's a guy dressed as Michael Myers and a guy dressed as Jason, and they both had knives." At the time, before everything going on with society, you could bring actual weapons in, and nobody cared.

"So I'm watching these two guys and they bump into each other, and they turn around; they square off and are in character," Ripple continued. "I'm thinking 'Ok, here we go.' I started moving to where my weapon is. The next thing, they started apologizing to each other; they're falling all over themselves. 'Dude, I'm sorry. It was my fault.' 'No, dude, it was my fault. My mask, I couldn't ...'"

Ripple goes on to explain it just clicked. Horror fans aren't bad people. He added he found horror fans to be the nicest, most down to earth, most generous people he has ever met in his life.

Scares That Care became a natural fit to bring out the good of the horror community as a whole, and more importantly show people who don't enjoy horror these people are just like them; they just enjoy a different genre of entertainment.

So, it became something Ripple really wanted to try. The first check went to the Johns Hopkins children's cancer ward. After which it became a matter of what he could do to make a true impact or make a change. To keep everything legitimate and everything above board Ripple reached out to Johns Hopkins.

"I said this is who I am, this is my plan, this is what I want to do. May I have your permission to collect on your behalf, because I didn't want anybody calling them saying 'Hey, this guy Joe Ripple with this organization called Scares That Care is collecting on your behalf,' and they don't know anything about it," he said. "That would've been

See STC, page 14

STC, cont. from page 13

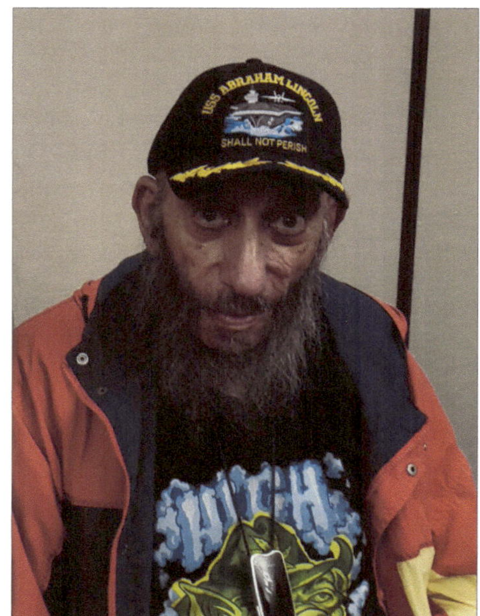

Sid Haig at Scares That Care 2018. Sadly, Haig passed away Sept. 21, 2019, not long after STC 2019. *Photo by D. Pardee Whiting*

bad."

After receiving an official letter giving STC permission to collect on their behalf, Ripple started a Facebook page, and the first 12 people to like the page were his friends from HorrorFind. As of Oct. 26, the STC page has 223,000 followers.

Once the organization met the goal set for Johns Hopkins, he moved on to the Kennedy Krieger Institute where Ripple's former partner's daughter was treated. "I wanted to do something for them," he said. From there STC moved on to raising donations for Make A Wish.

However, Ripple began thinking that while it was a good thing these organizations were receiving money from horror fans, the families it was helping had no idea who was donating the money. This led to him deciding to make STC a 501(c)(3) organization in 2007.

He said he made the decision to "adopt our own families; let's raise money and give the check directly to the families so that those families know that money came from the horror community."

This way the families know people outside of the doctors and other medical caregivers are supporting them and care about them. However, because STC wants to ensure the funds go to someone in true need each of the three families adopted every year have to go through a background check.

"Because you know, there are people unfortunately who fake illnesses. You have to be able to provide ... not necessarily medical documentation because I don't want to violate HIPAA [Health Insurance Portability Accessibility Act], but I have to know who's treating you," Ripple explained.

It is a matter of what is the issue and where the person is being treated. Part of that issue is being able to show a true need for help, somebody who hasn't had a GoFund Me campaign for $200,000, Ripple said, adding they are looking for someone who is under that radar.

Each year STC adopts three families and raises $10,000 per family. He acknowledges that is not a lot of money; however, Ripple said it is a lot when faced with several hundred thousand dollars in medical bills and the emotional toll attached. STC wants those people to know it's not necessarily about the money; it's about letting them know they matter, and these strangers have come together to help.

Ripple and the board find families to adopt mostly through Facebook and through horror fans themselves. As Scares That Care grows, it continues to be supported by people who really want to help others, so it becomes word of mouth.

Ripple admits they would like to be able to help more people, but it is one of those situations where you can't help everybody. "At least we can help three."

It can be disconcerting, though, because the people STC can't help will get frustrated and Ripple will get a lot of bad emails. He said he doesn't take it personally because it is about the situation at hand.

Ripple continued doing things on his own until 2011, when the 501(c)(3) was official and he added a board of directors, along with state representatives. In addition to being non-profit, it is 100 percent volunteer run and operated. No one in the organization, including himself, receives a paycheck.

"The board recently changed, but when I initially launched the board I wanted it to be as inclusive as I could possibly make it. In all of this the inclusivity of what it means to be a true charity was important for me in the aspect of I didn't want it to be so stoically mundane, as it were," Ripple said, adding, "That was not necessarily the primary reason; I wanted it to be individuals from a wide variety of backgrounds because I wanted to do good in the world. Now with looking back, with all the things that have happened since, it's definitely important to have

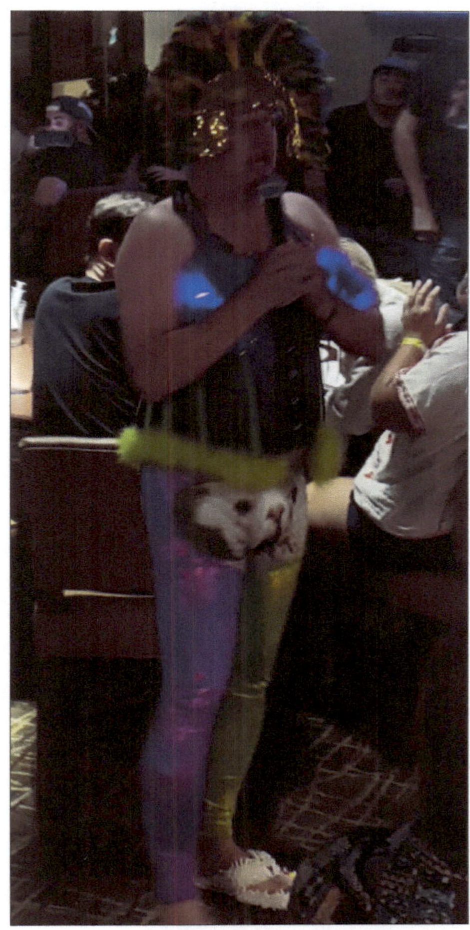

Scares That Care founder Joe Ripple says a few words during his annual Bra Walk for "tips"at Scares That Care 2019. The annual walk raises money for a breast cancer survivor "adopted" by the charity.
Photo by D. Pardee Whiting

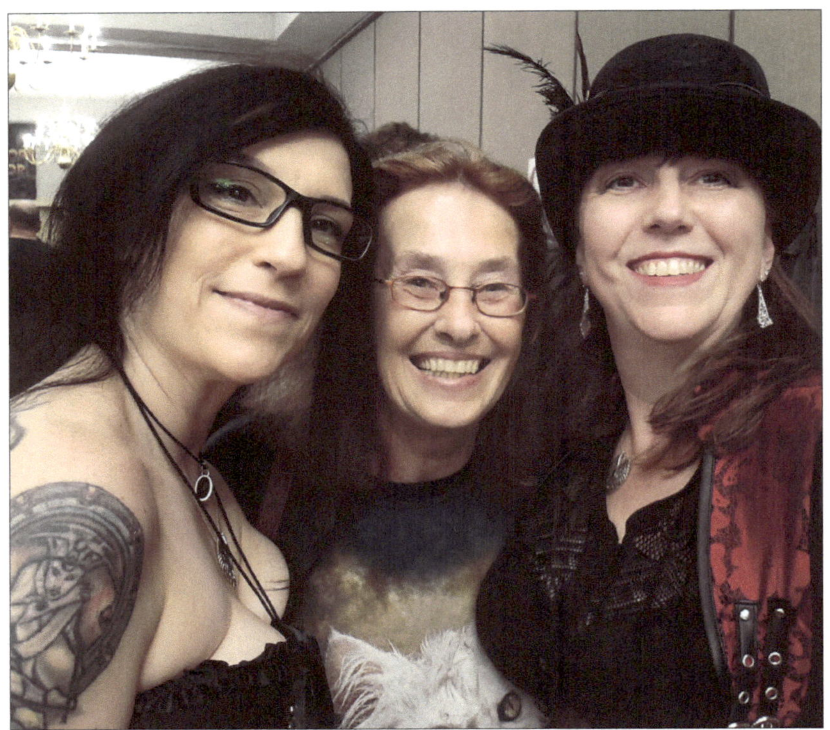

Lisa Vasquez (left) and Donelle Pardee Whiting (right) of Stitched Smile Publications meet one of SSP's fans, Joan Macleod (center) at Scares That Care 2018.

that inclusivity."

With STC's growth it came time to create its own family friendly convention. According to Ripple, members of the organization were spending an inordinate amount of time away from their families and money out of pocket to travel around to different conventions. Looking at what they were trying to do and what they wanted to accomplish it was a lot of work, a lot of time away from jobs with a lot of time off requests.

A state rep would say they could cover a certain event, and "all of sudden something would happen and they wouldn't be able to attend," Ripple explained, adding it became more prudent to start their own convention.

However, STC still goes to other conventions. For example, they are the official charity of Mad Monster Party, so they will always attend those cons, along with Creature Feature Weekend and Rock and Shock. Ripple said they used to attend Carolina Fear Fest, and there are always conventions popping up and sending an invite.

"We do our best to go, but to continually try to go to all of these conventions was beginning to be too much," he said. "We decided we are established enough we want to pick an area where there wasn't any other convention because we didn't want to create drama."

They tried it the first year in Williamsburg, VA and were, in Ripple's words, "somewhat successful." Knowing how conventions thrive on word of mouth and how people are treated they were able to move into year two, three, and four. "We've been growing ever since."

With that growth came the decision to expand and add a spring convention in April 2020 in Racine, WI. Unfortunately, the Racine event had to be postponed because of COVID-19 and the ensuing lockdown. The minute the lockdown began, Ripple cancelled Scares That Care-Racine.

"We do this for money, but it is to help other people. People are more important than money," he said. "Another thing I did once the lockdown started happening, I put out a tweet and a notice on Facebook saying do not send us any money. Do not donate to us, because right now with everything that is going on I would rather you take care of yourselves. You can help me later."

He went on to explain while a lot of people say it was a tough call to make, he did not consider it so when you realize why the decision is being made. He told of how one of the organization's people is African-American and whose daughter is asthmatic.

"This virus has hit the African-American community much harder than the Caucasian population. I care about his kids as I do my own daughter. So if I were to put on that show and for some reason he were to catch COVID and he were to take it home," he said, "and give it to his daughter and she dies I couldn't live with myself."

He added the shows are great to go out and blow off steam and have a good time, but with chances of this virus spreading it was not worth the risk. The reason people go to STC is to help others. But it is also for the camaraderie, the friendships, the closeness, to drink, and to have a good time. Ripple sees it as he has to do what is best for everybody. That means assessing what is the potential risk.

With COVID lockdown continuing into the summer, Ripple made the decision to cancel Scares That Care-Williamsburg, held the first weekend of August every year, as well. This decision was made in May rather than wait until the end of June. He said he worked with both hotels, and the staff at each were phenomenal to work with. For Williamsburg, Ripple spoke with the hotel's general manager to get a feel for the situation and what, if anything, to expect from the hotel.

Ripple said he was told not to come because the general manager was not even sure he would have a staff available to make sure the convention was successful. "At that point it was a no-brainer. Let's pause this thing. Everybody just take a break for a year. We'll be back together next year in 2021, and we'll have just as much fun as we would in 2020," he added.

The hotels made arrangements to transfer reservations to 2021 for those who want to keep

See STC, page 16

STC, cont. from page 15

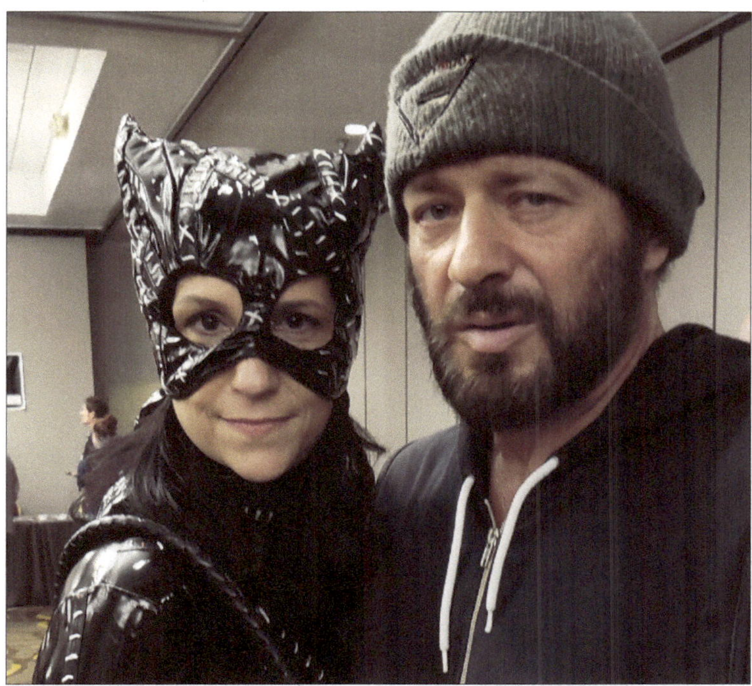

Catwoman (Lisa Vasquez) takes a moment to say hello to Costas Mandylor at Scares That Care 2018.
Photo by D. Pardee Whiting

their rooms. To this end, Ripple is busy working closely with the hotels to make sure everyone is taken care of.

In order to give STC participants an outlet, Ripple and the board create a one-day virtual convention. Viewers could participate via Brian Keene's YouTube channel by posting questions during the panels. Actor Pruitt Taylor Vince (*Constantine*, *Bird Box*, *Touching Evil*) and special effects makeup artist Roy Wooley (*Face Off Season 5*, *Black Panther*, *Zombieland*, *The Hunger Games: Mockingjay Part 1*, *The Hunger Games: Mockingjay Part 2*), who were scheduled to appear in Williamsburg, were on hand for the virtual con.

As for special guests, i.e. celebrities, Ripple said as much as STC wants people to meet and greet stars, money is a key factor. He does not see a point in paying a high cost if that means a family goes without. He added he is extremely grateful for those stars who do come and participate.

"We're very, very happy they're there."

In his opinion, conventions popularity declined when conventions bring in mega superstars, but attendees have to pay an enormous amount of money just to get into the event. Then once you have your turn to meet your favorite star, you're in and out in three seconds. To Ripple, that is not any fun.

"So, why not scale back a little bit, bring in celebrities people want to meet, but at the same time don't overwhelm the attendees so they're still [able to shop] the vendors; they're still going to the panels, and they're still attending the Q and As. They're still attending a wide variety of the other options [the escape room, the video game room, the auction, etc.] that we have, and they don't have to take out a second mortgage to do it. We try to plan our events so they are economically fun for everybody."

> *I'm an ordinary guy who came up with an idea.*

Along with vendors, the activity rooms, and auction items convention goers can expect a Halloween costume parade for kids. In addition, at the end of the second day, Ripple will do a bra walk for donations where he will dress up in drag and walk through the event.

He explained on Facebook it started out the first year when they were auctioning off a bra that was going to be signed by every celebrity in attendance. "I thought what better way to advertise the auction of the bra than to put it on and wear it into the [hotel] bar. People started tipping money, and now all of the money collected during this walk each year goes toward our lady fighting breast cancer."

The bra walk has become more lavish over the years, but Ripple figures if the ladies fighting breast cancer can go through that, he can embarrass himself for a few extra donations.

Some celebrity guests in the past include Sid Haig, Keith David, Costas Mandylor, Mark Boone Junior, Tommy Flanagan, Kim Coates, David Labrava, Jenette Goldstein, Sean Patrick Flanery, along with many others.

Celebrity guests are not just limited to movie stars, however. Authors Josh Malerman, Jonathan Maberry, James A. Moore, Jeff Strand, Wrath James White, Jonathan Janz, Paul Tremblay, and others have also put in appearances.

Ripple, who goes by the moniker Llamafather, thanks to his likeness being compared to a llama, does not like to be the center of appreciation. He said he may have founded Scares That Care, but he would rather applaud the hard work of those who help it continue and grow.

"I'm an ordinary guy who came up with an idea. If you have a problem then you come to me. If you want to give thanks, give the thanks to the people who are supporting me and who are doing all the work. I do a lot of work myself, but I am the quote-unquote face of the charity, and I hate when people tell me thank you for doing something because I am a very small piece of this. In all of this there are so many people behind the scenes who are doing an extraordinary amount of work, and I want to make sure they get recognized."

Scares That Care can be found online at https://scaresthatcare.org/home and on Facebook at https://www.facebook.com/ScaresThatCarePage.

Fertilizer

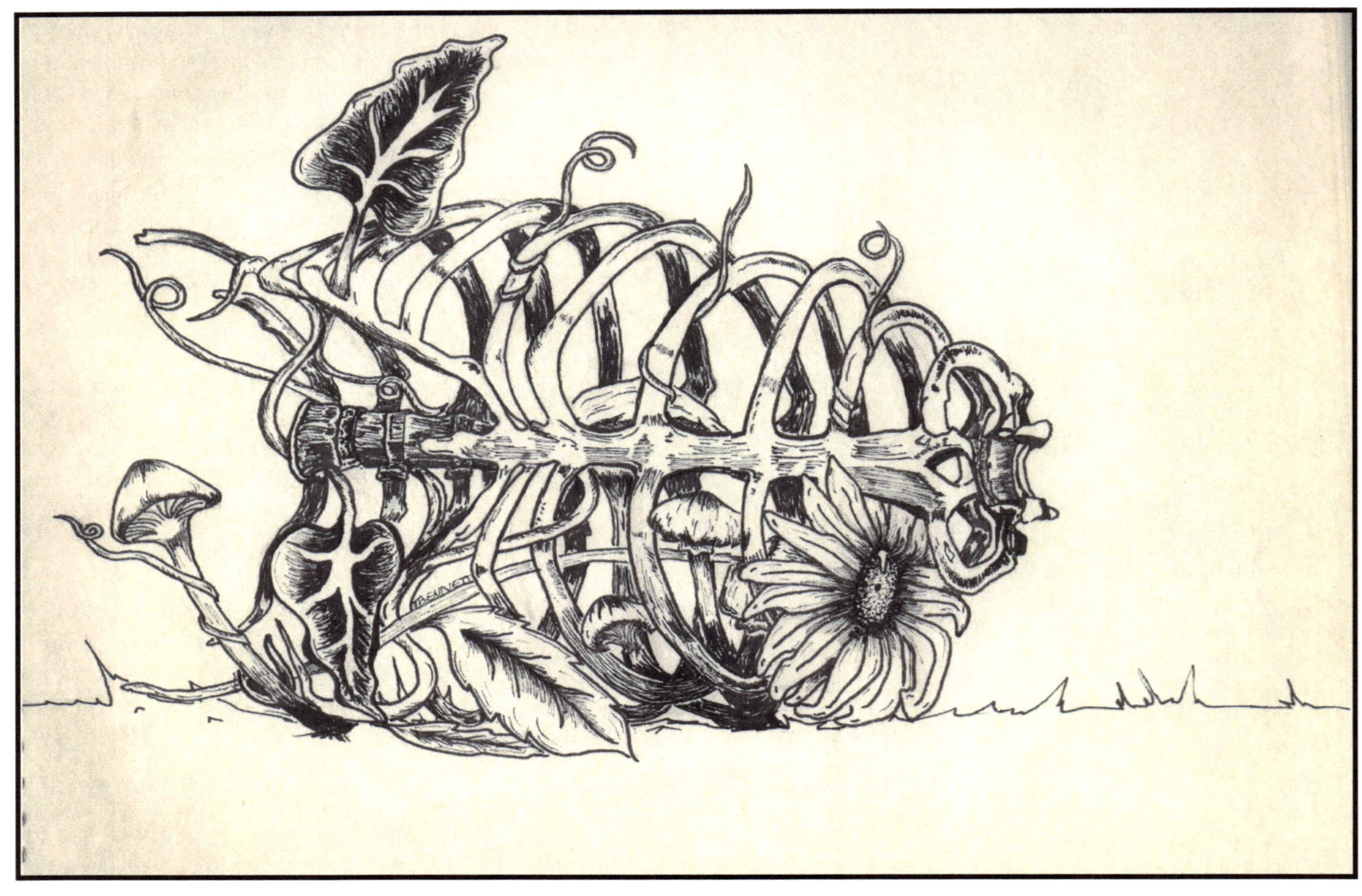

By Tara Bennett of Darque Pixie Designs / You can find more by Darque Pixie Designs on Facebook at: https://www.facebook.com/darquepixiedesigns

The whole idea of being mesmerized and not in control of your own actions is fascinating and a little spooky. I remember hearing about someone who'd gone to a magic act, and a person in the audience had become hypnotized by observing too closely what magician was doing on stage, and thought it was spooky to lose your consciousness that way.

~Chris Van Allsburg

BEHIND THE BLINDFOLD:

Up close and personal with Josh Malerman

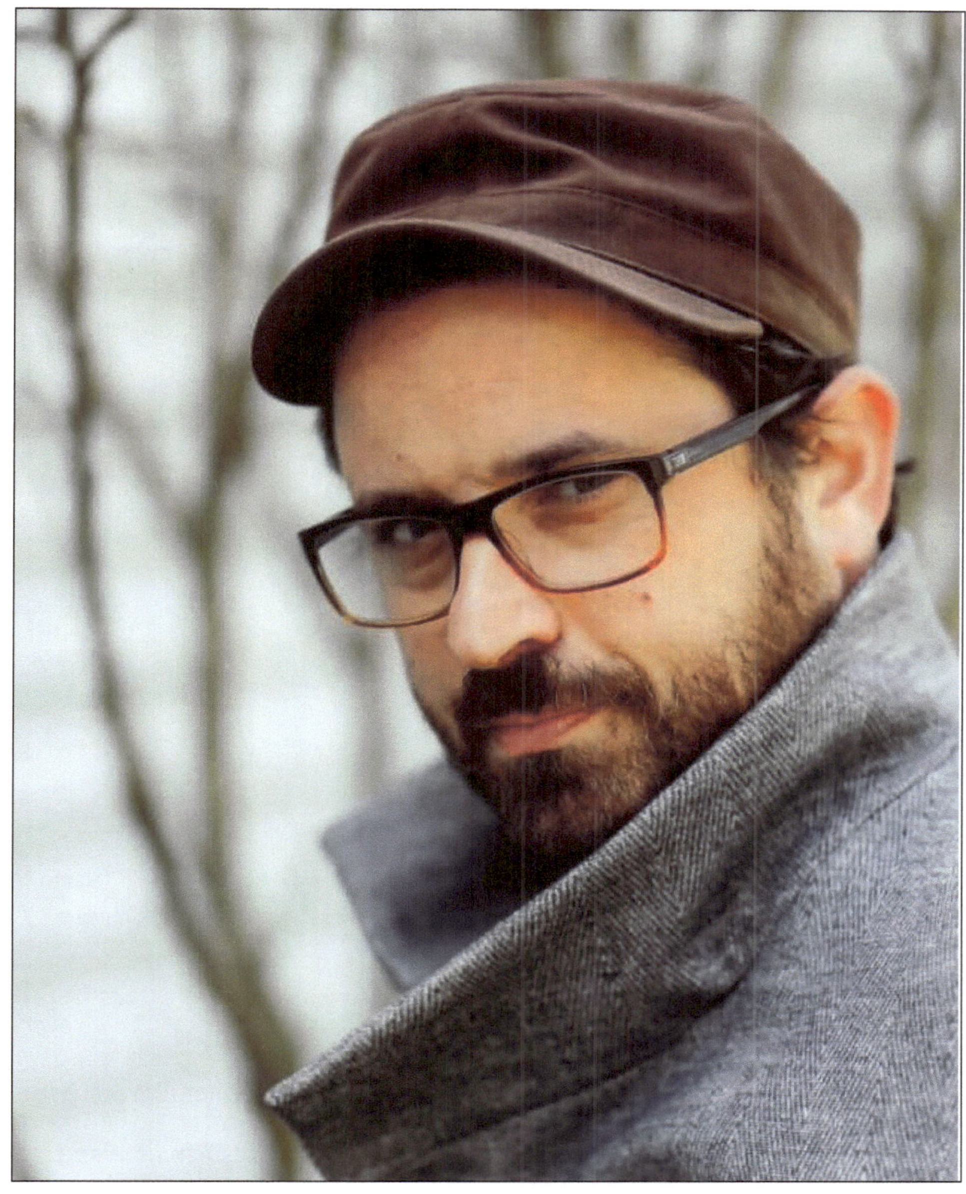

By D. Pardee Whiting

"The Luck You Got" isn't just the theme song for the Showtime show *Shameless,* nor is it just something Josh Malerman wrote for his band The High Strung; some people may consider it to be what helped launch the best-selling author's book career. However, it is more hard work, persistence, discipline, and a bit of good timing that led to his current success.

Malerman is evidence of what happens when you have a passion, that passion becomes a dream, and with perseverance it becomes reality.

Described in one interview as an aging hipster, Malerman is full of energy, and yet, is able to focus on what is in front of him and consistently churn out written works of art while wearing his trademark hat, jacket, and boots. The outfit, he said, is more of his uniform and came about through interactions with people while on tour with The High Strung.

"The whole thing is ... I always, almost always have cowboy boots, and it all started when the band hit the road, and this is like years ago and objects just started falling into place," he said. One woman told him he should try a certain type of pants. Another girl told him he should try cowboy boots. "And a friend ...," he added, while touching the lapels of his jacket, "this jacket didn't fit quite right, and another friend was wearing one of these." Malerman touches his ever-present painter cap style hat. To some it may appear piecemeal, but he said one day he decided it was his "uniform."

Malerman added he always tries to dress in that uniform when he writes, but he'll also wear it at other times. "Like here we are doing an interview; I didn't know if this was going to be video or not. I just like to ... I don't know ... it puts me in the right state of mind."

Despite being sought after for several interviews of late—thanks to the recent success of his debut novel *Bird Box*, which was released as a Netflix original in 2018, and most recently its sequel *Malorie*—he remains open and approachable, like a longtime friend.

Malerman remembers a time before *Bird Box* was published, when he and his bandmates were on the road with another band. He told them he was writing a book. One of the guys asked what it was about, so Malerman told him.

"He was like 'Oh, you write scary horror novels.' [He couldn't] imagine me as a *Fangoria* reading guy because I'm in this very bright, upbeat band." Malerman said. "Not like Sha Na Na, but still it's a bright upbeat band."

To him the words come from the same place. Rock 'n' Roll and horror. They're both from a similar, playful place, he explained, but the books are a lot darker.

Malerman attributes his introduction to horror to his uncle, "my mom's brother;" although, he has not seen him in a while.

"I would love to talk to him about

this," he said. "We would all hang out at his house, my brothers and me, my cousins. Playing basketball, and my uncle's like 'Josh, I think you'll like this movie,' and he put on *Twilight Zone the Movie*. I must have been 10, 11, 12. I don't know what I said that made him think I would like this movie."

Malerman added it was quite the introduction to horror because it covers the various types of stories that can fall under the horror classification. The movie leads off with the prologue starring Dan Ackroyd followed by the first story segment that is a social commentary with Vic Morrow as a total racist nutjob forced to live in the bodies of minorities and experience the type of hate he dished out. The second is the heartwarming "Kick the Can." In the third segment anything goes, the kid who can imagine anything, he said. Then there is the fourth story, the creature feature, the monster on the airplane followed by the wraparound with Ackroyd asking "if you want to see something really scary, which is the scariest part of all."

"So, for me, it was like a full spectrum education, the first time I watched a horror movie, and I saw so much variety," he said, adding. "I think that it's no coincidence that I hear from people that each of my books, they all seem like their own thing. They're all totally different from each other."

One would think someone who was introduced to horror at a young age and writes horror novels wouldn't be a scaredy cat, but Malerman would prove you wrong. For example, while talking about his fiancé Allison Laakko, Malerman glanced up at the door to his office, swore, and jumped, putting his hand to his chest.

"She was staring around the corner," he explained. "You saw the genuine fear just then. Yeah that was the real deal."

So aside from Laakko spooking him, what else scares Malerman? According to him, haunted houses. It doesn't matter if it is the fake ones meant to be entertaining or the real ones that likely harbor spirits. Either one will mess him up.

In terms of books, movies, more like the fictional realm, and even ghost hunts and such, Malerman said what

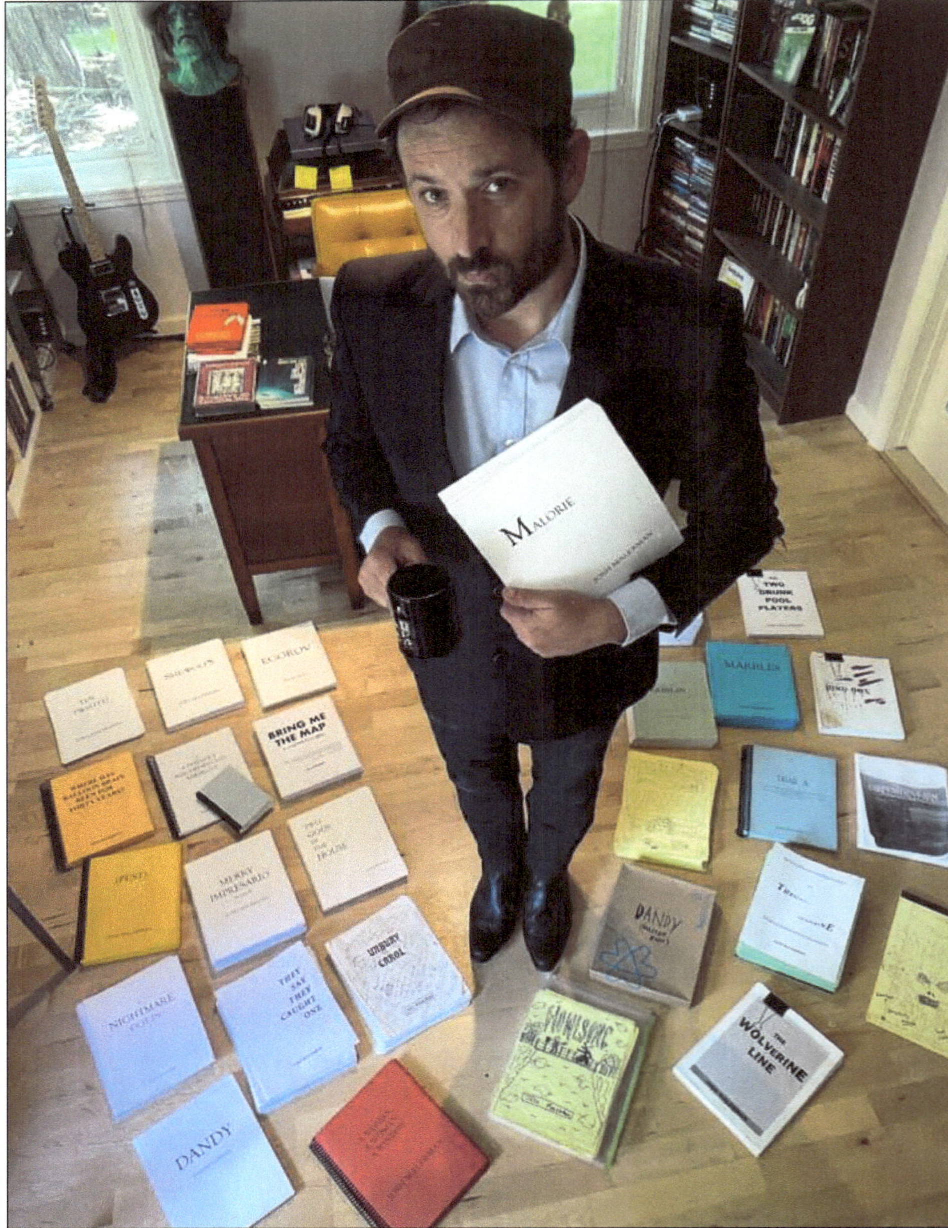

really freaks him out, "which is weird," is demons and witches. "Things that could ... entities that could take control of you. Make it so you are out of control versus a stalker who I would have to do physical battle with or something."

Laakko's fear trigger is opposite, he said, adding she is 100 percent afraid of the person watching through the window, the stalker. "I guess Jason [Voorhees], where I am more afraid of *The Exorcist*. The irony there is Allison was raised ... her dad was a pastor, just retired, was a pastor his whole life. She was raised with religion, and she watches *The Exorcist* and [she] and her dad ... I watched it with both of them, were laughing at how stupid it was. And I'm like what, I'm scared out of my mind."

According to Malerman he is sort of a neurotic dude, and said when he watches something with a stalker, he thinks it's nothing. Meanwhile, Laakko, he adds, is totally freaked out. "It's interesting."

He said he thinks he is more afraid of losing control and likens it to the same fear he has of a drug like acid or something that can be all encompassing. "I don't like the idea of being gone."

For him alcohol is not something that makes him feel he has lost all control of who he is or feel possessed.

See JOSH, page 20

JOSH, cont. from page 19

He considers it more of a personality enhancer; although, he admits to knowing a few people who have been "possessed" by booze.

But it's that sense of both feet off the ground, whether intentionally with a drug or whether by a demon or entity type of possession. "That fucks me up."

"I've always been more afraid of the unseen rather than the seen."
~Josh Malerman

He mentioned one time they went on a ghost hunt in the Stanley Hotel in Estes Park, CO—made famous by Stephen King's *The Shining*—and there was a story of a woman who claimed something followed her home from the hotel. She ended up quitting afterward, he added.

And that, he said, was the kind of thing, kind of story, that is too much for him. There are certain things Malerman said he can't watch alone; for example, movies like *The Conjuring*. "The movie *Paranormal Activity,* like, wrecked me when it came out. And a lot of my friends were like 'That was so stupid. It was like just footprints and stuff like that.' But I was like totally freaked out by it. So, yeah, I've always been more afraid of the unseen rather than the seen."

Although it is the unseen that scares Malerman the most, he has other fears he managed to get under control thanks to his relationship with Laakko. At one time, he said, he used to be afraid of flying. He doesn't know for sure why it happened, but several years ago they went on a trip to Brazil. He said coming home he was fine, until he wasn't. He added he doesn't know why he had a "freakout" moment, but after that trip he became so afraid of flying he didn't board his flight when he was scheduled for a panel with Joe Hill, Paul Tremblay, Kat Howard, and Thomas Olde Heuvelt back when he only had one book out.

Malerman was all set to fly to Boston. Laakko dropped him off at the airport. He got through security and to his gate. Eventually it was time to board, and he got in line; however, once it was his turn to board, he turned around and left the airport.

"I wasn't deciding or anything. My turn came up, and I was like nope, and I left," he said, adding, "I called Allison, was like hey, I didn't get on the plane." She told him there was probably another one. "I'm like no, no, no, I'm not going. I'm not going on a plane."

Malerman's agent was not happy because the panel was a good thing for him, and he needed to get over not wanting to fly. He said after that he realized he thought the ordeal was because Laakko wasn't with him. She has a calmness to her, like it's not a big deal and "fuck it, it's fine," he elaborated, saying it is not that she is good luck. "She's a really great travel companion."

He admits he isn't sure if that was the problem, but he does know it took a bit before he got on a plane again. Now Malerman almost looks forward to flights because it is the only time he is okay with someone else being in control; he has no choice but to have a drink and watch a movie or something.

"When I'm at home I'm always thinking, like, should I be writing, should I be doing this, like constantly de, de, de, de, de," he said with the staccato sound of a pretend machine gun while shaking his finger toward his temple. "I don't really do much in [a plane] setting, so it's like, all right you take the wheel. I've learned to actually like it. I've gotten over that one."

The author said he finds it interesting we say things about being scared of things like spiders or of flying. He added he didn't know those fears can change until Laakko opened his mind to things like spiders and such.

Malerman calls Laakko a full-blown naturalist; she loves all things in nature. He told a story of how Laakko, who is from Michigan's Upper Peninsula where there are crazy spiders and other things, took a handful of non-poisonous snakes, "and other things like that."

She opened his mind to it's just a little bug, "and she even touched the back of one," he said while pantomiming touching something small and creepy looking, "and I'm like ... oh, geesh," he added with a shuddering shake of his hands. "But then it's like seeing her do this ... it's worked. I'm less freaked out by spiders."

Another instance of working through a fear was when Malerman got a handle on his stage fright when it came to public speaking. He was hired to give an hour-long speech on writing at a university. "Leading up to it I'm pissing my pants, chewing my fingernails off, taking notes on writing, like what am I gonna say, I got to talk for an hour? Imagine [being] in front of a room alone talking for as long as you and I have been talking."

Two days before he was scheduled to speak the dean called Malerman and told him they would like him to talk about the spirit of writing rather than the mechanics of writing. He said that was it for him. He was done and pretty much got rid of his notes. Malerman added he didn't even reference the notes. He found he could talk about the spirit of writing all day. It was a subject he knows well.

He told himself it wasn't a book report, nor was he doing a history presentation. He would be talking about books and writing. He got up in front of the room and started. The first time he looked down he saw it had been 45 minutes which, he said, did something for his stage fright. He still gets nervous; although, once he gets started, he likes it.

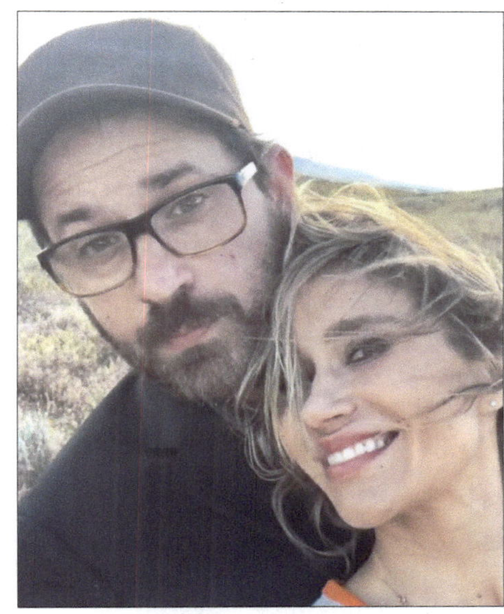

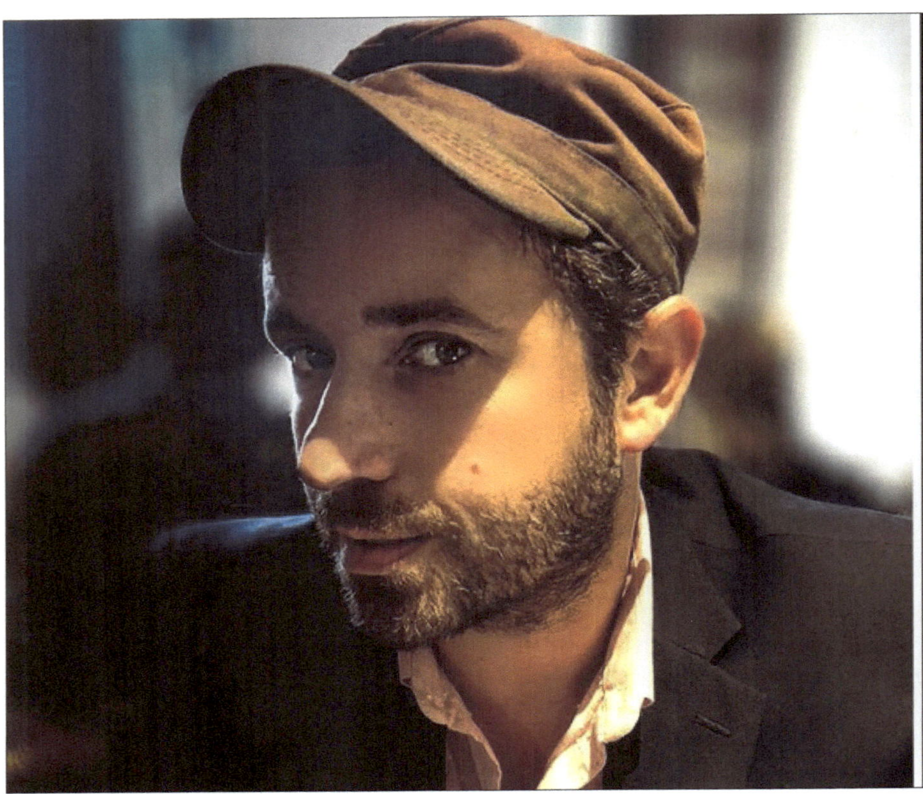

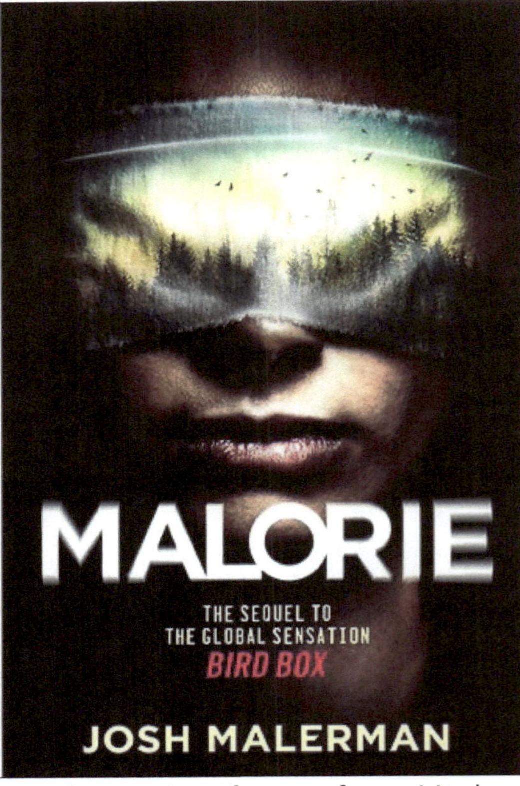

"I was a little nervous even about this interview today. And once it started, I was like let's go, let's go, let's go."

This is what makes Malerman so approachable. He gets scared. He gets nervous. But he isn't afraid to admit it happens. He mentioned his first experience with a convention of any sort that was in 2014, about a month before *Bird Box* was released. Harper Collins sent him a box of 60 hardcovers he could sell while at the event.

He was seated at a table with his books on display, and he had a sign where he had written his name. He said he sat at the table looking around, not knowing anyone, and no one knew him. Before long he decided to write "Free Hardcovers" on the sign, stood up, and handed a book to everyone who walked by.

"I started to meet people. Because I'm now the guy who started handing out free hardcovers. I started to meet all these people. I was like 'Holy shit, this isn't just like I'm here selling books or giving them away. This is meeting people I relate to, yeah, and it was like a whole mind-blowing moment for me."

When he was younger Malerman had a more literary group of friends, a couple of whom would not necessarily make fun of the horror genre, but they would look down their nose. They would say things like, "Oh, you're like in horror. We were reading Joyce together. We were reading Virginia Woolf together. What are you doing?" he said.

"So for me to encounter people who were totally jazzed by this too ... I didn't even know they were out there," Malerman continued. "I mean, how could you not know in 2014? I don't know. I didn't have a cell phone until I was 30-something. I wasn't on social media until I was older than that. So for me, it was somewhat astonishing to discover thousands of people who are not only into this, but have read thousands of books in this genre."

Laakko wasn't just a calming influence on Malerman's nerves and fears, he said, but she also opened his mind to more in life. He added he was always into classical music, but "Allison has opened a gazillion doors to me. She plays classical guitar. She can really sing. I'm used to years with my friends; we all have whiny dude voices." He laughed before continuing. "So, from word one it was astonishing for me to be ... intimate with someone that could really, like really ... like at the opera house or at any stage anywhere."

He admits it became a little mind-blowing to see Laakko isn't just pretty or funny or free spirited. She plays piano in addition to guitar. She paints, which is "off the charts." There's her athleticism, which he said is also off the charts.

Malerman shared the time Laakko went running, and he followed her on his bicycle because "I can't keep up with her no way." He timed her run, and at the end he told her she ran 3.1 miles, a 5K, and her time was "like sick." He looked up 5K times for Michigan and found, with her random run, she would have placed second or third in the state championship.

He hesitates to use the word talent, he said, because sometimes it implies there's no work involved. It implies they were born into something. However, he admitted Laakko is made of different stuff than he is; he doesn't know exactly what it is. "I feel like I'm scraping along with every letter, and she's a natural at a lot of things.

At some point while he was talking Malerman's Weimaraner, that likes to be close to him whenever she can, came into his office to say hello. The author proudly introduced Valo and showed off her bed next to the full bookcase behind him. This led to the subject of Laakko's affinity for wildlife.

See JOSH, page 22

JOSH, cont. from page 21

Malerman affectionately told the tale of the ducks. Tuli, the couple's Vizsla, brought two eggs inside after being out. Laakko was still asleep, he shared, and he decided to take the eggs back outside. Then Tuli brought in a third, and by that time Laakko was awake. So, she took the egg from Tuli's mouth.

"Allison is a total, total nature person ... an animal lover." Malerman explained. "Not just lover, like super informed and intelligent about it. She was staring at the egg for a while, and I was like oh, God she's gonna try to hatch this thing."

Laakko went outside to get the other eggs. She determined one wasn't going to survive. She did her research and bought an incubator. However, Tuli had punctured one of the eggs when she originally brought it inside, and it did not survive. The other egg did and hatched.

"So, now we've hatched an egg, and we have this duckling. But, ducklings don't like to be alone, so we ordered two more ducklings," he said. "[These] ducklings came in the mail in these boxes with these holes. They seemed fine."

In order to keep the ducklings safe until they were older and separated from the dogs, they were kept in a fenced in dog run the previous owners of Malerman's house had. As all creatures do, the ducklings grew, and the original duck Laakko hatched is believed to have joined a gang of ducks that visit the pond behind the house. The author said the duck would fly away regularly, and they saw it with the other ducks. But then the flock left.

They come back occasionally in different group dynamics, he said, and Laakko thinks she has seen it. "But that's sort of the goal. [You] rehab it. You find this egg, and you get it back into the wild. But Allison also spent weeks and hours in the extra bedroom and outside with the ducks, and so it's actually an emotional thing for it to leave the nest."

Malerman's demeanor calms a bit as he talks about Laakko; there's genuine affection in his voice and a softer

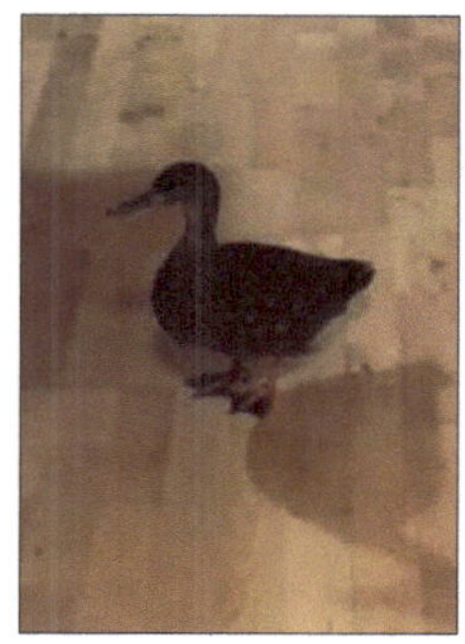

facial expression.

The two met after a record release show for the album *Posible O' Imposible* by The High Strung, of which "there's some amazing live video footage, which was used in [his] recent CBS interview."

"We were wasted and having all this fun, and afterwards the drummer, who is one of my lifelong best friends ... he was kinda walking me out because I was kinda drenched and drunk," he said. "And then this ... it almost seemed like a fairy or sprite or something, but she was almost as tall as me, just appeared all eyes and legs and dark hair at the time under this hat."

Malerman had face paint on under his eyes in football player fashion. He described how Laakko walked up to him and told him she liked face paint too and asked for some. He reached in his pocket for the Sharpie he had used, and she grabbed his face. She rubbed one cheek against his and then again on the opposite side.

"And I was like ..." He gasped before continuing. "What just happened?" Laakko asked if it worked, and he admitted it did. They have been together ever since.

"She may have instigated it, or she may have started it, but I fucking knew before she did that this was the real thing! I will take this to my grave, and in the earliest of early days I told her this is no question 'you and me, this is it.'"

She had recently broken up with someone, but Malerman said he was willing to wait because he didn't care. "This is it, like let's just roll. Come on. OK, take a few months if you want. It's gonna happen either way," he said he told her.

"She definitely started it, but I saw it first."

Although the couple has not set a wedding date, Malerman said there should be one. However, with the whirlwind of books and the production of *Bird Box* and its subsequent release on Netflix, it's all still new. He said there's no pressure, but when he met Laakko he didn't have a book deal yet. That happened a few weeks later.

"Now we have all the time in the world, but it's also a pandemic. So, not sure, but no pressure, but yeah, I love the idea."

Speaking on COVID, Malerman is often asked about a parallel, or connection, to Malorie and her insistence of wearing the blindfold in his best seller *Malorie*. He admitted to not being tired of answering those questions. "That's one of the beauties of all this happening a little bit later in life. I didn't get a book deal until I was like 37 or something. I don't think I'm ever going to get tired of answering these questions."

He smiled and chuckled before continuing. "Because it's all so much like holy shit, I can't even believe

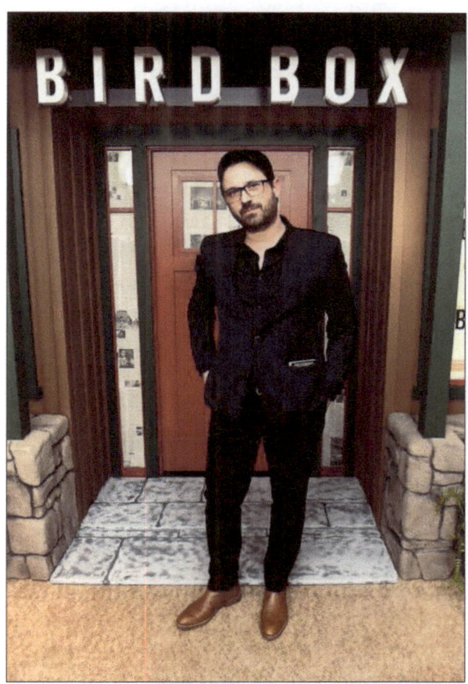

we're talking about this. How fucking awesome. I definitely see the parallel, obviously between she's staunchly blindfolded, and I in my life, I'm all about the mask. But the huge difference here is that Tom, who is, he's not anti-blindfold; he's beyond the blindfold. He's not saying 'Mom, your idea is dumb or phony or fake or weak,' whatever. He's saying we can do better than this."

Tom is trying to bridge the gap between the new world and how Malorie describes the old world. "By being progressive," Malerman said, adding, "in a way both are progressive." Tom is all about new ideas. It's complicated to compare Tom to modern day politics. The parallel gets shaky in Malerman's mind because Tom wants the old world for good reasons, but Malorie is strict about wearing the blindfold.

"What really links Malorie to the modern, or the *Bird Box* scenario to the modern world, is the not knowing when it's going to end. The creatures arrive suddenly. It wasn't from a lab. There's no vaccine for the creatures. So, to me if they arrived as suddenly as they did, couldn't they go away as suddenly as they came?"

The characters don't know why the creatures showed up and if they left or not. Could it be a period of observation? Have they seen enough and done enough? To Malerman this would be a super interesting novel because they're gone, or you think, or you hope they are all gone. Maybe they left one thing behind or something. "Mom, look. I've got an alien in the backyard," he said with a laugh.

So the bigger parallel for Malerman to what's happening now is more along the lines of when is this going to end. "Is this ride over? No, we're still going. Ok. I can write another novel at home now."

Malerman said lockdown hasn't been too bad, though, as several key people in his life arrived at a good place in their lives prior to sheltering in place.

For example, his brother got a really good job. His friend Mark got a job as a teacher full-time rather than part-time. Another friend moved into a new house, and another friend had a baby right before the pandemic hit.

Malerman and Laakko moved into their house just outside of Detroit, not far from where he grew up. "We had been living for four something years in a much smaller place in a sort of cityish area called Ferndale. And we ... if we were still there during the pandemic, I think I would be losing my marbles. I would ..." Malerman stops briefly as Valo checks on him.

"So, I think I would be losing my marbles if we were still there, and I would be tempted to go up the street to the restaurant and to the bars and stuff." With the new house, which Malerman calls a Godsend, there is a huge yard for the dogs and plenty of space.

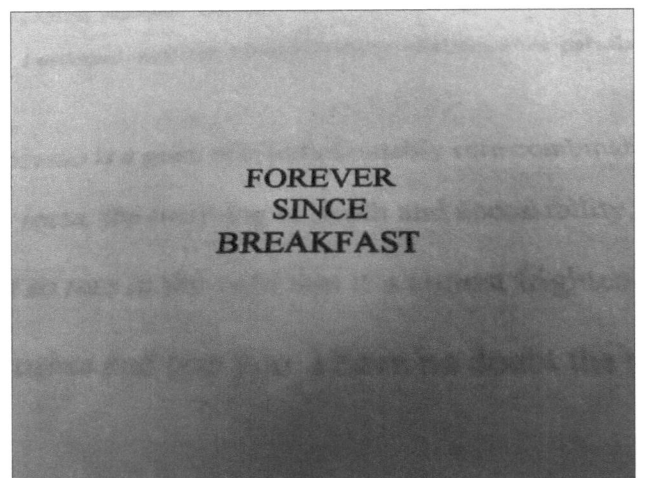

Even with hatching and raising ducks, feeding deer, both Malerman and Laakko have been able to keep busy. Malerman has written two novels, one of which, *A House at the Bottom of A Lake*, is scheduled for a January 2021 release from Del Rey. It was originally published with This Is Horror. In addition, another book, *Decorum at the Deathbed*, is available now as an Audible Original. He said having finished two novels in six months is not so much a testament to how fast he works as it is a testament to how long society has been dealing with the pandemic.

Two novels in a short period of time, one of which he was in the process of rewriting at the time of our interview, is pretty good, he said, adding it is almost a sense of why not now. He has also been using the time to go through his to be read pile rather than going to the bookstore. And Laakko has done "a gazillion projects I know she has wanted to get done."

Malerman also took time out to binge watch *The Umbrella Academy*, and he "freaking loved it." He added *Outlander* to his binged list. "Allison read the whole series, all eight books. That series is sweet. It's really ... wow!" he said. "And it gets really dark. In that first season there's some shit in there you have never seen before, believe you me. There's some stuff in there that's not even in horror movies."

He and Laakko also watched *The Marvelous Mrs. Maisel*, and he said, freaking love it. Add in *Lovecraft Country* and a binge session of *Deadwood*, and you have Malerman's guilty pleasure.

"I've never been a watch TV for hours kind of guy. Every so often I'll do it. I start to feel a little guilty if I watch too much TV.

Even with all the distractions and work getting done, there is still a little bit of cabin fever; though, Malerman attributes it to having a heated Presidential election campaign happening at the same time as the pandemic and its resulting lockdown. One on its own is rough, he said, but to have both it becomes a crazy moment in time. From his viewpoint the mood and what ensues following the election hinges on who wins.

Although Malerman like the Detroit Lions, he said it has been a weird time for sports. He said Laakko pointed out it's possible that more people are politically piqued because the seasons are not in their normal schedule and structure. So, before you would have people all about sports, but they were taken away for a while and they're back now, but in a different way. "It's an interesting thing to consider. How much tribalism there is because there isn't anything else you're rooting for."

Leaving politics for another day, Malerman said "we're here, we're loving, we're reading, we're writing, she's building, raising animals. [So] there's a lot to be okay about it too."

Speaking of his house, Malerman mentioned he grew up about four miles away in a suburb of Detroit and went all the way through high school there. He graduated from Michigan State University, and from there moved to New York City with his best friends, his bandmates. He said they

See JOSH, page 24

JOSH, cont. from page 23

lived in a place right under the Williamsburg Bridge right across the river from the World Trade Center.

"We actually saw the towers fall in person," he said, his mood turning somber. "That was wild, and it's always like a wild anniversary."

Shortly afterward, The High Strung hit the road to what amounted to about six and a half years of touring, which meant they didn't have a home base. They would stay with friends or family any time they were in Michigan for a month or more. It was during one of those months Malerman wrote his first novel.

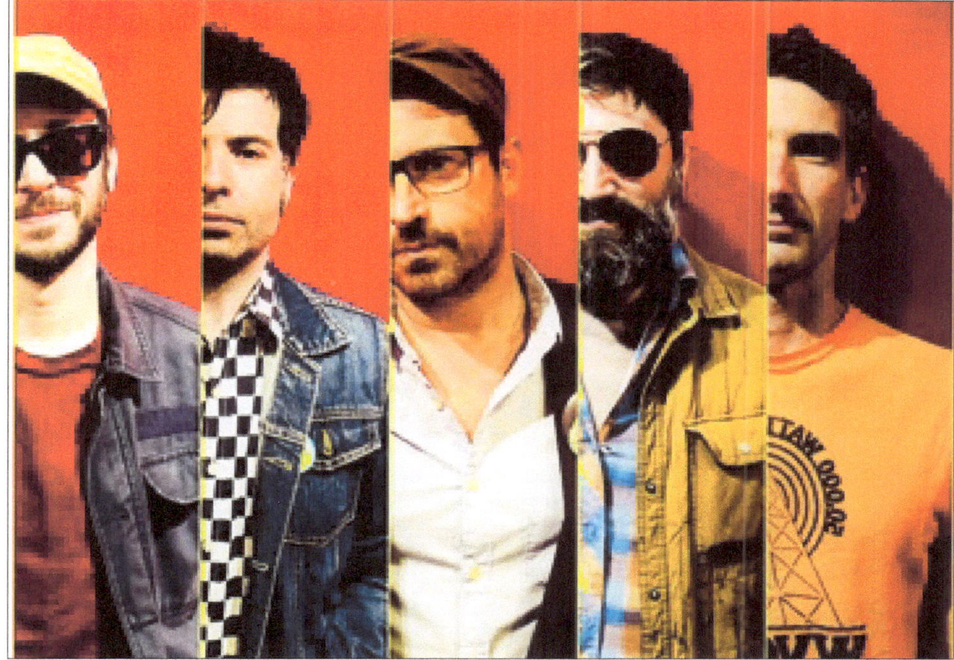

He said he had been trying for years and failed at it for ten years and four attempts. But when Malerman says he failed he means he didn't finish, he clarified. He didn't care if it was good or bad. He just didn't know how to finish. His breakthrough happened when he was 29 and home for two months.

"I went to this all-night coffee shop. I wrote from midnight to 4 a.m. I was surrounded by all these law students, which was amazing rather than, like an artistic group of people. And the reason it was amazing was that everyone was there to work. Everyone was there to study. Everyone's nose was in their books."

Malerman said he showed up and met a few people through that. They didn't talk about the government or Kubrick. They got to work, which he credits with opening his mind to the discipline side of writing. He added he already knew how to write and finish the songs for the band. However, there's a discipline to the marathon of writing a novel that he didn't see until he had one.

To be surrounded by people who daily, nightly, from midnight to whenever, pushed Malerman forward to finishing. "The place was full of people studying. I just sat there at a table alone and wrote freehand until it was done." That was 16 years ago.

With a pile of rough drafts piling up, lightening struck in the form of one of Malerman's high school friends, Dave Simmer, contacted him and put Malerman's book *Goblin* into the hands of someone who could put him on the path to best-selling author.

Not long after, Malerman had an agent and was on his way. *Bird Box* became a hit that went into production with Netflix and Sandra Bullock before the book was even published.

Malerman said when he was writing *Bird Box* he lived in an apartment, but it was more of a top floor of a house. During the first round of writing he had birds, finches, flying around his apartment. "And this is going to sound like the most literal thing you've ever heard, but it's true. At one point, I included them as the alarm signal, and I didn't have a title, and I'm halfway through."

Usually Malerman would have a tile right away, but this time he didn't. He said he looked down and next to him on the floor was the box the birds came in from the pet store. It was like a Matryoshka, Russian nesting dolls affect to him. "I could never have imagined in that moment how significant it made the birds to the story, because it's like the title and it's the imagery. So they were a small part of the story to me, but they symbolized a much greater thing."

However, when Malerman was writing Malorie he didn't think he needed a place for the birds in the story. "Then I was like, no, no, no. Let's find a place for them. And that's what led to insanity of a bird taking flight. Or the flock taking flight in Tom's mind that Malorie was worried about."

For those who have yet to read either book we will leave it there.

Nowadays, Malerman not only wears his trademark clothes, he said he writes three to four hours at a time while listening to a horror movie soundtrack on vinyl. "When I start a project, I work on it every day until it's done. Almost without exception."

One of his latest books he just finished, which should be released in 2021, is titled *Forever Since Breakfast*. The title, he said, is a line from a Charles Manson interview. He added he doesn't normally do something like that, but it was a quote that stuck with him.

During an interview a man asked Manson how old he was, to which Manson said he's not in the same timeline as him, that he's not even in the same world. The interview then asked how old Manson is in his world. Manson answered he was forever since breakfast.

Other areas of inspiration stems from what the author termed the prolific artist. For example, Hitchcock putting out a movie a year. Hitchcock's first five movies were silent, although not by choice. It was where the world was at the time. He ended up "doing a movie a year from the '20s all the way up to ... *Psycho* was 1960. And he's as old as the century. In 1960 he's 60. His heyday is *Vertigo*, *North by Northwest*, *Rear Window*; this is all mid to late 50s to 60s. *The Birds*, he's 63. That's wild. It's super, super wild. So, that's super inspirational to me."

Even though Woody Allen has become somewhat of an "odd subject," he still finds the director another inspiration in that he put out a movie a year since 1976 or something. Stephen King, the band God of My Voices, and in a slightly different way, Agatha Christie.

What Malerman loves about the prolific artist is watching them go through phases, watching their career arc. The bands in the '60s were putting out two albums a year, and you could literally watch them grow in real time.

Now it seems, he said, a band puts out an album every few years or something like that. This, in his opinion, puts more pressure to sound like the other albums that came before, whereas if the album were to release six months later the band has the creative freedom to try something different without losing that sense of who they are.

To Malerman this same type of growth can be applied to writers. He said he suspects writers sometimes get stuck trying to write their first novel because they may feel like the novel needs to represent them in full, as if it is their one statement, their one work of art, their one expression.

"It's the body of work that expresses you in full not that single work of art," he explained. "I sound like it could mean like 'Ah, who cares if that song sucks; the next one will be good.' It's not like that. It's more like let's just stay in motion; some are gonna be better than others just naturally, but they're all gonna be awesome in their own way. And remember the spotlight is disbursed amongst [the total] rather than a single thing, like this is how I see the world. This is what I think is scary. This is what I think is love. No, no, no. Let's spread that out over an entire career and all that pressure vanishes."

Malerman continued, saying it is a matter of just keep moving. We've all read books. Some of our favorite books have parts we don't like. For example, *The Brother Karamazov* is one of Malerman's favorite books; however, there is a section of about 100 pages where he admits he's almost falling asleep.

He added he was watching *The Godfather* movies the other day, and he couldn't believe how good the first one was. But there is one stretch where the character Michael, played by Al Pacino, goes to Sicily and Malerman found himself falling asleep. He acknowledges it is one of the greatest movies he's ever seen, but at that one part he had to tell himself it will get better. "Let's keep going."

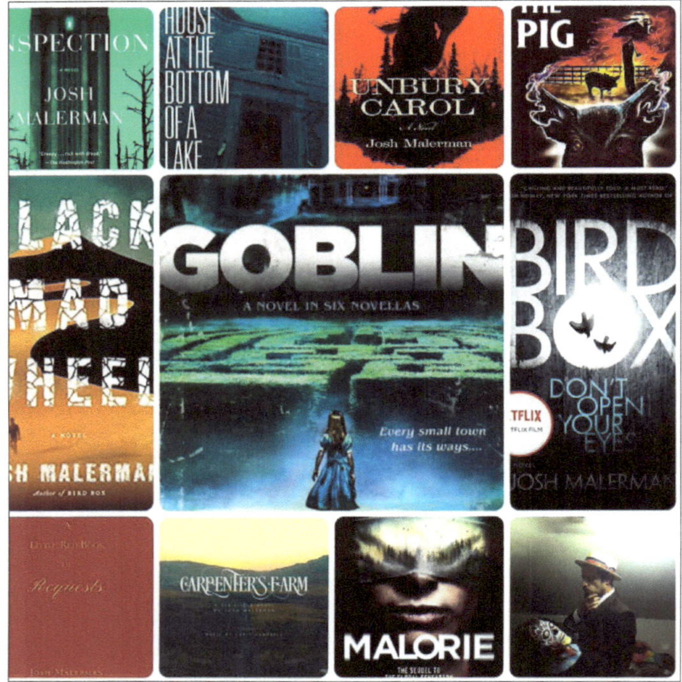

Malerman's way to keep going is to add a production company to his list of projects. He and his manager started a production company two years ago called Spin A Black Yarn, named after one of the author's short story collections expected to be out next year. The original idea was to find a home in film or TV for Malerman's books and/or stories, but it did not take long to expand to include stories from other writers in the horror genre.

While not wanting to give out too much information, Malerman did say they wrapped up shooting on the production company's first film as producers. This movie is based on a book from a known writer in horror, but he wouldn't say more. Yet.

> *"Josh Malerman proves his place among my all-time favorite authors of horror fiction."*
> ~Sadie "Mother Horror" Hartmann

However, as of Halloween 2020, Malerman posted an announcement on his Facebook page saying the first movie produced by Ryan Lewis and himself was announced in The Hollywood Reporter. The movie is based on a book by Max Booth III and is directed by Sean King O'Grady. In addition to Spin a Black Yarn Productions, the movie is produced to Atlas Industries, Peter Block, Donovan Leitch, Hantz Motion Pictures.

When it comes to the horror genre, there are those who are for, and those who are against, trigger warnings on books. Malerman's viewpoint is understanding of why someone would want them. "Some stuff is heavy. I do worry that certain triggers (perhaps nonsexual ones) could ruin the shock or surprise of a certain moment in a horror novel, but I think the trade-off is worth it," he said. "If it would bring a reader to relive something in a terrible way? Yeah, why not let them know beforehand. I get it.

Even with the busy life of an author, and now a producer, Malerman has not turned his back on his band. He still writes music, and The High Strung is recording two new albums. But just as important as putting together new music is, the discovery of an album recorded about two weeks prior to their debut album was exciting. This mystery album, he said, is much, much better than the band realized and is currently being mastered. He said they expect it to be released in early 2021.

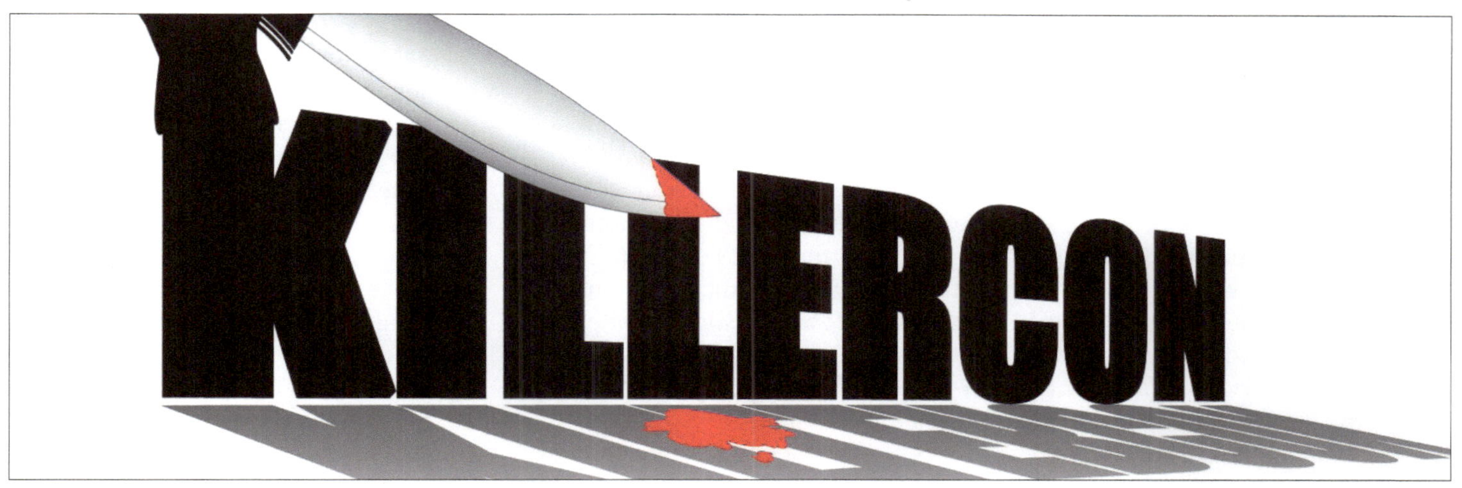

The Splatter Zone

KillerCon connects extreme horror fans

By D. Pardee Whiting

By definition, Splatterpunk is a movement within the horror genre distinguished by countercultural alignment and hyper intensive horror with no limits, and is known as a genre characterized by graphically described scenes of an extreme gory nature.

Coined in 1986 by David J. Schow at the Twelfth World Fantasy Convention in Providence, RI, Splatterpunk is regarded as a revolt against what is considered the traditional, meekly suggestive horror story.

The horror sub-genre is not for everyone, though, as some others draw a line between what inspires terror and what inspires nausea.

Despite its detractors, Splatterpunk is alive and well thanks to the authors who write it and their readers. Then there are the conventions that help keep the genre thriving. KillerCon, created by author Wrath James White, is just such a convention.

White, who lived in Las Vegas at the time, said he was at Necon—the Northeastern Writer's Conference—in either 2003 or '04, and "I was lamenting the lack of a writer's convention in Las Vegas. I was going on about 'I wish someone would start a convention in Vegas.'"

People told him there was one year when they had the World Horror Convention in Vegas and nobody went to any panels. They were all gambling and going the strip clubs, White said, adding they were all telling him no one's going to do a convention in Vegas, and proceeded to ask him why he doesn't start one.

Several people offered to help White start a horror writer's convention of his own. In the end it was down to Monica O'Rourke, who White met at HorrorFind, and White. KillerCon was born. White could not recall the exact year, but a search puts the first KillerCon in 2008.

The first and second KillerCon were held at the Palace Station Hotel in Vegas. From there it moved to the Stratosphere before settling in Austin.

"We had the first KillerCon; it was crazy. It was just outrageous, and some of the things we have done since, like having parties sponsored by publishers every night of the convention where all the alcohol is free," White said. "We charge a fee to sponsor the party; the fee is really to go out and buy alcohol."

When White first moved KillerCon from Vegas to Austin he was nervous. He said he feared KillerCon was Vegas. He wondered if that was what made KillerCon work because in Vegas it was a slightly different event.

"I mean, we had the casinos. There were times where I rented a limo and took all our guests of honor out the strip clubs. Vegas was a different event."

So when the con was moved to Austin, White was concerned with being able to capture the same energy without the casinos, strip clubs, and wildness of Vegas. However, he said, they succeeded. It's different, but it is still KillerCon.

Aside from the panels one can expect at a convention, KillerCon hosts several contests to challenge a writer's skill. The first year there was an erotic horror contest. There have also been creative fiction contests in which the judges give the contestants five words they have to use in a 300-word mini story.

"They have to use all five words. The judges come up with some of the most incongruous words. But it's amazing; you would think they would come up with some ridiculous stories, but we get some of the most creative and imaginative stories utilizing these ridiculous words," White said, adding, "They do an amazing job. It's crazy. I have [tried]; I couldn't do it."

The first prize in this contest is

usually 50 bucks, and White explained what he considered great is for a lot of people this represents their first professional sale.

Like any con, things evolve. When World Horror (currently listed as defunct) stopped doing gross out contests and it disappeared entirely, KillerCon took it on because of its popularity. One of the first recognitions White earned was his controversial second-place win at the 2002 World Horror Convention in Chicago.

"Everyone thought I should have won, but that was kind of like my coming out party," he explained. "It was one of the most highly anticipated events at World Horror, and then they decided they were above it and got rid of it. So we picked it up."

From there the gross out contest became one of the most popular events. After that, KillerCon started getting crazy with contests. In the third year, the Wings of Pain was added. Authors would have to eat progressively spicier hot wings and answer questions. They would have milk and bread, and the minute someone would grab the milk they're out.

In 2019, the convention coordinators introduced a new contest called One Punch from Wrath. According to Stitched Smile Publications CEO Lisa Vasquez, it was a convention participant who came up with the idea. White said they got a lot of heat for it, because if you're not there it sounds horrible. However, the people at the event all loved it.

"They laughed their asses off, and it was wonderful thing."

People who just saw videos of White punching people would say it was terrible because when taken out of context everything at KillerCon appears ridiculous and outrageous. Within the context of the convention things look more normal.

"You gotta understand," White said, "I like to say KillerCon is the reunion of family you did not know you have. We all get together, even with the people where this is their first KillerCon, we quickly become family. If at the end of the weekend you haven't made a new friend you have missed the entire point of KillerCon. It's being around friends and family [and] having a good time."

The rule of One Punch from Wrath is simple. Participants are asked questions about the weekend's guest of honor and about the Splatterpunk Award nominees. If someone gives the wrong answer, they get a punch in the arm. However, some people think that's a terrible game. White's answer to that is the people who feel that way should never come to KillerCon.

"Clearly you don't get it," he said, adding, "It's not for you. If you think this is like the worst thing in the world then you're not family." With a laugh he continued. "The thing is there are plenty of conventions where you can go and be literary and keep a distance from the fans and sit behind the booth and sign autographs and be the superstar."

"I like to say KillerCon is the reunion of family you did not know you have. We all get together, even with the people where this is their first KillerCon, we quickly become family."
~Wrath James White

But KillerCon is not that type of convention. It is different. Not just in the types of contests and how it caters to those who prefer the Splatterpunk type of horror, but also in its schedule.

KillerCon has one track programming so attendees never have to decide between seeing someone read and a panel or whether to go to a contest instead. It's one track so everyone moves together, from a reading to a panel to a contest, etc.

There is no separation between the guest of honor, the most popular famous authors, the readers, new writers, and everything else. Everyone hangs together all weekend. They party together all weekend, and they eat together the entire weekend.

In addition, White "always tells new writers … we don't have pitch sessions. We did that for two years, and it was just silly. You're going to be eating and drinking with these publishers and editors and so on and so forth."

White's thinking is, if writers can't sell a story to someone they are eating with or getting drunk with, spending an hour or so with them, then a five to ten-minute pitch session is not going to help. So, they eliminated that from the convention.

KillerCon attendees are already hanging with the authors they love and have been reading for years. They're hanging the editors and publishers they've always wanted to sell a story to, and they are doing so all weekend.

"So, if you have questions that you wanted to ask Edward Lee, he's right there; ask him. If you have questions you wanted to ask Brian Keene, he's sitting next to you. Ask him. That's what KillerCon is. It's getting rid of the separation between all of us. It's one big party. One big family. One big reunion."

White said he finds it funny seeing people go up to Joe Lansdale, and they're all nervous. There are so many people, even some of the more famous people. They spend so much time in front of a computer that when they come out and party they're also nervous as hell. At least, the first time. After they come out to their first KillerCon, White continued, they're like "Hey, I'm with all the socially awkward peeps. These are my people."

As if all the fun, games, eating, and drinking were not enough, KillerCon also holds the Splatterpunk Awards, which Schow helped put together conceptually. In its first year it was emotional enough to surprise Brian Keene.

Part of that emotion stems from the Jeff Gonzalez Lifetime Achievement Award as a memorial to the author who passed away in 2014.

The rest of the emotion comes from Splatterpunk and extreme horror being largely ignored when it comes to awards for writing. "We hadn't realized Ed Lee had never won an award. Thirty years of writing and he had never won an award. Ours was the first award he ever won. It was an emo-

See SPLATTER, page 28

SPLATTER, cont. from page 27

tional moment. It wound up we didn't realize how important these awards were to people."

White went on to elaborate on why he believes KillerCon's Splatterpunk Awards are so important.

"Literary folks treat 'genre writers' like genres are like these ghettos where they send their least talented authors. And then when you do break out and you're acknowledged for your talent it becomes literature," he said. "You still write the same stuff, but because now it is getting lauded by critics, and so on and so forth, now this is literature, this is literary horror. Like what is literary horror? Literary horror just means that critics liked it. That's all it means."

Unfortunately, this year's KillerCon, like so many other conventions, fell prey to COVID-19. After White made the call to cancel KillerCon 2020, it did not take him long to decide to go the virtual route. He said it was an ethical decision to cancel the event. He didn't want to be responsible for anyone getting sick or losing their life.

Regardless of how much money was already spent, and regardless of how much money they were never going to see again, White did not want to make it a financial decision when it came to people's health and safety.

"So, I decided to cancel and eat the money that was lost."

On the tails of that decision came what he called a crazy decision. One he did not talk with his wife about first. He told her he was going to do KillerCon as an online event, and he was going to do it for free.

To say White's wife was not happy at this news is an understatement. She was angry at first because he did not mention it to her before committing to the plan and announcing it, he explained, adding he thought it was the right decision.

People were hurting, he said. People were having issues with depression and issues with loneliness and so forth. White did not want to profit from that, he wanted to help people rather than make a buck off them.

White only charged a nominal fee to the vendors for their ads, "which were phenomenal; those ads were amazing," and that was only to lock down some type of commitment.

"I've worked other conventions before, and it's crazy to me that you have track down and hunt people down to give you their ads. A lot of times they will give you the money months in advance, and then you're like okay where's the ad, and you get it two days before the event."

When he announced the convention would be online and on Zoom, White said, "people said then you can't do the contests." His response was to say yes, they can. When they asked how he would be able to do Wings of Pain on Zoom he replied, "Watch me."

The sealed hot sauces used for the contest were shipped and had to remain unopened until the contest was live. Viewers would then watch the contestants open the bottles. In full view of the online audience they were told exactly how much to put on each wing and then they ate them.

He added he thought it would be hilarious because they were planning on having two sauces from last year that almost "killed" people.

Irish Spike sponsored the contest, and according to White, they're sauces are amazing and delicious.

The contest kicked off with the delicious low heat sauces, and the participants were commenting on how good they were. Then they switched to hotter sauces, going from about 10,000 on the Skoville scale to about one million. White couldn't help but laugh as he remembered their reactions and comments of it tasting like Satan's ass.

"It was awesome," White said with a laugh.

People even questioned how White and company would pull off the gross out contest. "Are you kidding me?" was his response. "That's easy. They were asking if we were going to have people record video." He told them no, that it was going to be live. Participants would read their stories live, and if they had props they can do it from their screens, no problem. "It went off really well. I was happy [with the result]."

The Splatterpunk Awards were also no less of a success, according to White. The only concern he had prior to the event was if they would be able to get the same impact, the gravitas of the moment, and be as powerful in emotion as they had the first time. And the second time.

"So that was important. We announced that next year John Skipp would be the recipient of the Jeff Gonzalez Lifetime Achievement Award," White said, adding he read *Light at the End* when he was about 14. Skipp is another Splatterpunk author who has never received an award for his writing before, despite decades of published work.

Even though the virtual format for KillerCon was a learning experience, White said he would do it again if COVID-19 should force the issue. He added they learned a lot pulling it together and getting through the day.

The great thing about KillerCon, according to White, is there is not a strict formula. "I always say I am a stew maker not a cake maker. I throw things together and let's see how this works. That's always been the joke with KillerCon; people are always like 'Wrath just decided the week before to throw a party."

That, he said, is how it looks, but it takes a year of planning. So, when putting together the virtual event there was a scramble. Literally a week before the event White realized people didn't know which time zone to follow. He said he had to get busy and promote that the programming would be Central time.

He added he hadn't thought about if you're at an in-person event you're automatically on whatever time zone where it's hosted, so organizers don't have to specify. Plus, in person there are wranglers whose job it is to get people where they're supposed to be when they're supposed to be there.

When it's online and someone isn't logged on you have to hope you have their phone number to call them, he said, adding he had some numbers but not all of them. If they didn't see the note from the Monday before and only had the information from two months prior and hadn't checked for updates, they could potentially miss their panel or reading.

White takes full responsibility for all the little glitches, because this was the first time doing a virtual event. He now knows to get everyone's accurate, up-to-date contact information, and make sure time zone questions for the programming are sorted well beforehand.

It is a learning curve, he noted, but not unlike hosting an event in person. "People attending don't see all the fuckups. All they see is the final product. If they have a good time then it's all good."

Despite this year's KillerCon being on Zoom this year and having a few bumps, White considers it a success. One thing he said he appreciated was at the in-person event he has people to whom he can delegate, but for the virtual event it was all him. Although, he did admit he does like to be in control, he is thankful to everyone who takes on a lot of the needed tasks. But even with the help he will still run around and step in to get things done when needed.

People who missed the event and want to check it out will find it was not recorded. White said he prefers not having recordings of any of the awards, panels, or readings even at the in-person event because he doesn't want presenters to feel inhibited. He wants everyone to be natural, spontaneous, say whatever the hell they're feeling, do whatever they're feeling.

"That's what KillerCon is about."

So, if you're horror leans to the extreme and gory with extra splatter, and you want to see KillerCon for yourself you will have to plan on attending.

You can follow KillerCon on Facebook at https://www.facebook.com/KillerCon-Austin or online at http://www.killerconaustin.com.

A BIT OF TRIVIA

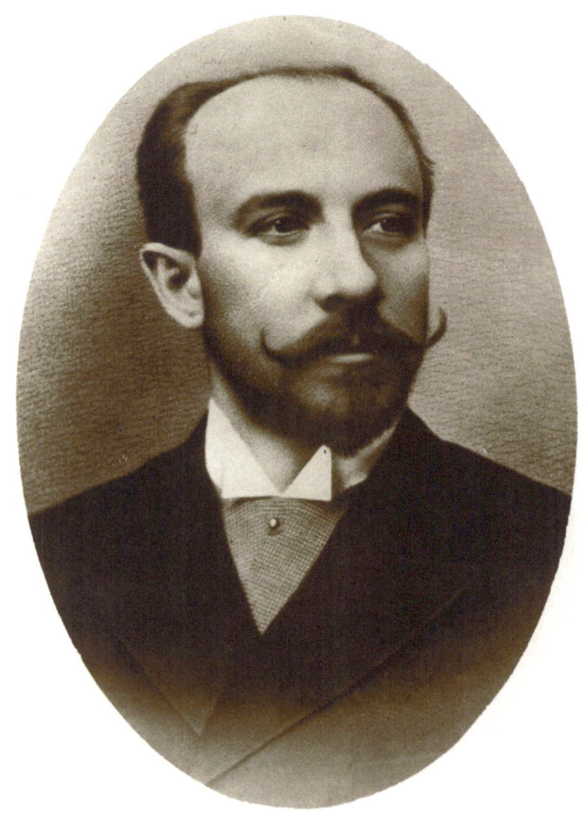

Did you know …?

Director Georges Méliès' 1896 silent film, *Le Manoir du Diable* (*The House of the Devil),* is regarded as the first horror film. However, Méliès is said to have intended the film's bizarre imagery—including a bat turning into a man—to be funny and whimsical. This element led some observers to label the work as the first vampire film. He intended to evoke amusement and wonder rather than fear. His pioneering use of trick photography to portray the supernatural backfired and has some calling him the first horror director. In addition to Méliès' directorial style, the film was innovative in length with a run time of more than three minutes, which was ambitious for the era.

According to the book *Universal Monsters: Origins* by Christopher Ripley, what was notable about the film was the director's use of cinematography to morph characters into other characters. Although technology did not exist to create such visuals, he used limited tools and his imagination to create a relatively impressive production.

Méliès' film depicts a brief pantomimed sketch in a theatrical comic fantasy style and tells the story of an encounter with the Devil and various attendant phantoms. It was filmed outside using painted scenery in the garden of Méliès' property in Montreuil, Seine-Saint-Denis, according to the book *L'Oeuvre de Georges Méliès* (*The work of Georges Méliès*) by Laurent Mannoni and Jacques Malthête.

The French film was released in Britain as *The Devil's Castle* and in the United States as *The Haunted Castle* and was thought lost until a print was discovered in the New Zealand Film Archive in 1988. A remake, also made by Méliès and often confused with the original, was made in 1897 under the same title, *Le Château Hanté* (*The Haunted Castle*).

There are no credits available as film actors performed anonymously in Méliès' era. According to *L'Oeuvre de Georges Méliès*, the film was released by his studio, commonly known as the Star Film Company.

"Where there is no imagination there is no horror"

~Sir Arthur Conan Doyle

THE ELEVATOR

By Ezekiel Kincaid

"Welcome to the Grand Casino and Hotel, Mister Lucas, glad you will be staying with us again," the tall, lanky man behind the front desk said. He wore a blue blazer and khaki pants.

Quinton Lucas.

Even his name screamed "douche-bag." He had money and success—everything a man needs to get along in this world. Quinton was fortunate he had money and success because he was ugly as hell.

"Thanks, Raul, always good to see you," Quinton said in his grav-el-laden voice and placed his bags down at his feet. He stood just under six feet, with a large belly and bald-ing head. He wore a thick, peppered mustache, and his bushy eyebrows resembled black caterpillars resting above his eyes. His forehead wrin-kled when he talked, and his nose was the most prominent feature on his face.

"Mister Lucas, if you would, please follow Joshua. He will take your bags and get you on the eleva-tor." Raul shuffled some papers and smiled.

Quinton rolled his cigar to the oth-er side of his mouth "Joshua? What happened to the smokin' hot girl you had … oh, what was her name …?" Quinton snapped his fingers. "Oh yeah, Sophia?" Quinton raised a bushy eyebrow.

Quinton told his wife and kids he would be out of town this weekend for work. But instead, Vegas called his name. Mr. Lucas had a big week-end of gambling, drunkenness, and adultery planned.

Raul gave an apologetic nod. "I'm sorry Mister Lucas. We had to let her go last week. It seems her extra-curricular activities were carrying over into her job."

"What does that mean, Raul?" A perverted smile appeared Quinton's face.

"Take it to mean whatever you wish, Mister Lucas." Raul grinned and rapped his fingers on the desk.

Quinton snickered then turned and followed Joshua onto the elevator. "Joshua, huh?" Quinton folded his arms and scowled, working Joshua over with his eyes.

Joshua boasted a few inches on Quinton. His eyes were a deep brown. His skin was olive, with a well-manicured beard and short brown hair.

"Yes, sir, at your service." Joshua bowed.

Imagine with me, if you will, we have just paused this story like a movie mid scene. You are now star-ing at Quinton Lucas as he scowls while Joshua is in mid bow. From what you know about Quinton, you look upon him with a bit of disdain. But there is more.

Quinton was born in Houston, Texas and talks with a thick south-ern drawl. He graduated from the University of Houston with a con-centration in business and finance. It's where he met his beautiful wife Cecilia. Yes, regardless of his looks, Quinton landed a rather lovely woman. Ah, young Cecelia, her beauty would make the gods jeal-ous. Her father Ted owns the larg-est Mercedes-Benz dealership in the state. He took Quinton under his wing, and the rest is history.

It'd be nice to say with a wife this hot, an ugly duckling like Quinton would be a monogamous man, but if that were the case, there would be no story to tell. In fact, it's quite a regular habit of Quinton's to explore other pastures. Pastures he has to pay for, for sure (at least most of the time). Speaking of money again, be-cause Quinton is now part owner of Ted's car dealership, he can afford two extra homes—a summer home in Castle Rock and a winter home in Boca Rotan. All this success has made Quinton's attitude as big as his belly.

Kids? Sure, he has children. Two to be exact. Devan, twelve, and Ad-die, nine. Does Quinton care? Sure. He cares about doing what needs to be done to save face in their eyes. He buys them stuff, so he doesn't have to spend time with those "an-noying little bastards," as he is so fond of calling them.

The befuddling question is how can a guy like Quinton still have his family intact? The answer is simple. Quinton knows how to read people. He knows what to say, how to say it, and when to say it. His wife has no idea he cheats on her because he knows just what to do to make her feel appreciated. She also thinks all those out of town trips are work related, especially with her father covering for Quinton. The kids? They're easy to please. They love the stuff their father throws at them. But what about Quinton? Why does he stick around? Maybe it's because Ted, though retired, still owns part of the dealership. He's waiting for the old man to sign everything over to him and then croak. When that happens, Quinton plans on getting the hell out of Dodge.

Quinton does not appreciate life.

"Well, Joshua, you're not as nice to look at as your predecessor, but as long as you get me to the right floor and don't tear my shit up, we will have a great relationship." Quinton chuckled and rolled his cigar again. He pulled out a lighter, lit up, and puffed away like a locomotive.

"Of course, sir. I will make sure you get exactly what you need." Joshua stacked Quinton's bags nice and neat in the corner of the elevator.

"Well, right now I need you to get me up to the twenty-first floor so I can get ready. I got a big night ahead of me." Quinton made a thrusting motion with his hips and belted out a hearty laugh. "Know what I mean there, Josh? Huh? Huh?" Quinton gave Joshua a brisk pat on the back.

Joshua ignored him and pushed the button for the 21st floor.

"So how do you like this gig, Josh?"

"It's good. I get to meet a lot of people and hear a lot of interesting stories."

"Seen any crazy stuff yet?" Quinton exhaled the smoke from his cigar and glanced over at Joshua.

"Oh, nothing out of the ordinary yet sir, but I have a feeling that will soon change." Joshua stared straight ahead.

Quinton gave another belly laugh, then patted Joshua on the back again. "Hee hee hee, ya damn betcha, Josh. Ya damn betcha, boy."

The elevator stopped, and the bell dinged.

"Looks like we're here, Mister Lucas." Joshua turned his head in slow motion to look at Quinton.

"Yeah, yeah." Quinton reached into his coat pocket to grab a few bills to tip Joshua. The doors opened, and Quinton turned around to exit the elevator.

The scenery was not at all what he expected

"What the hell? Is this a joke, boy? Cause if it is, it ain't funny." Quinton peered out the doors and saw the front steps of his summer home.

"This is no joke, Quinton," Joshua said. His tone was as steady and serene as a trickling brook. He watched as Quinton ran his fingers through his thin hair in frustration.

"Ha Ha, Raul. Very funny!" Quinton raised his hands to the ceiling and turned toward the security camera. "What, is this some new state of the art crap for some new security system or something! And how did you get a picture of my home?! You better start talking Raul, or I'll sue your ass!" Quinton grew more annoyed. "Not funny! I have to meet someone across the street in 45 minutes! I ain't got time for this, you bunch of assclowns!"

Joshua reached out and placed his hand on Quinton's shoulder, "Quinton, this is no joke. Watch."

The elevator seemed to move like a carnival ride, or it stood still and the events happening in front of them moved like they would on a movie screen. Quinton couldn't tell which.

The two of them approached the front door. It opened to reveal a staircase. To its left was the sitting room, and to its right was the dining room.

"Quiiinton!" a voice called out. "Time for me to feed you your lunch!"

Quinton and Joshua went through the dining room and into the kitchen. Quinton's wife, Cecilia stood at the stove and stirred a bowl of tomato soup. She turned around and walked straight towards them.

"Cecilia," Quinton cried out. But she passed through him like a ghost.

They followed her back into the dining room and up the stairs. Once they reached the top of the stairs, they headed down to the end of the hallway. Off to the right they saw a doorway.

"Why, that's my room." Quinton rubbed his chin.

"Here, honey, it's time for your lunch," Cecilia said in a voice that could stir any man's heart.

They eased into the room, and Quinton saw himself sitting in a wheelchair. "Joshua! What the hell? You better start making sense of this shit right now!" Quinton turned around and faced the back of the elevator, and the doors shut. His mind spun like a merry-go-round, and his pulse pounded harder. He'd always been quick tempered, and if people didn't start talking, he aimed to start dishing out the consequences.

"Quinton, I know this is upsetting, but if you will please calm down I will explain everything to you. This is not a joke. This is not a projection from some fancy state of the art equipment. This is not your imagination, and Raul has nothing to do with this. This is real."

"But that was me … my house, my wife." Quinton's breathing got heavy, and he began to pace back and forth. "Get me out of here, Joshua. I've had enough of this shit. I'm going to make some phone calls, and by the end of the day I'll own this place. Take me back to the lobby."

"You can't go back, Quinton."

"What do you mean I can't go back, boy!" The vein in Quinton's' forehead pulsated. *Who does this jackass think he is? No one tells me no, especially a damn bellhop.*

"Let me explain. Are you ready to listen, Quinton?" Joshua crossed his arms.

Quinton wanted to punch Joshua in the nose, but he refrained. "Yeah boy, you best start talkin'." Quinton stopped pacing and looked Joshua in

See ELEVATOR, page 32

ELEVATOR, cont. from page 31

the eyes. Quinton's cheeks flushed and sweat beaded in the wrinkles of his fat forehead. "You best start spittin' it out!"

"I know all about you, Quinton. You have an amazing wife, adorable children, and loads of money. Yet, you cheat on your wife, neglect your kids, and treat people like scum. You come here at least twice a month to engage in a lifestyle that would make Caligula blush."

Quinton's eyes narrowed, and he clenched his fist.

"Quinton, you do not appreciate life. So, here's the deal. Each of these twenty-five floors contains an alternate reality; a reality you must choose. You cannot go back to the life you had. Your wife, your kids, your job—all will be different. In some of these realities, there will be no Cecelia and no children, and in some there will. Oh, and Quinton." Joshua held up a finger. "You have one hour to make your decision. If you do not make your decision, one will be made for you."

Quinton had it. His rage erupted like a volcano. "Bull. Shit. This is a crock! This isn't real. This kind of crap doesn't happen! Get me off this elevator now ..." Quinton looked down. "Give me that phone, asshole. I'm calling the front desk."

Joshua handed Quinton the phone. "Go ahead, Quinton, call. See what happens." Quinton picked up the elevator phone and called the front desk.

Nothing but static.

"You disabled the phone didn't you, you sick son of a bitch." Quinton slammed it down in its case.

"Now, now, Mister Lucas, there is no need for name calling. Try your cell." Joshua motioned with his head at Quinton's pocket.

Quinton pulled out his cell and dialed 911.

"Well, Quinton?"

"Nothing, I got nothing!" Quinton slipped his phone back in his pocket. He glared at Joshua, wiped the sweat from his eyes, and spat his cigar to the ground. Then, he lunged at Joshua with outstretched arms.

Joshua stepped out of the way. Quinton thudded into the corner and fell to one knee. Joshua saw his opportunity and moved in fast. He sank a guillotine choke hold on Quinton and squeezed. "Mister Lucas, violence will get you nowhere. This is the way it is. The only way out is to choose a floor. No amount of yelling, cussing, screaming, or fighting will make it any different." Joshua cinched the hold tighter, and Quinton tugged at his arm. "Quinton, I know you are so used to getting your way and this is hard for you to come to grips with, but this is not going to be your way. It is going to be as I say, understood?"

Quinton let out a grunt.

"Now, Quinton, calm down, and I will let you go." Joshua felt Quinton's body yield to submission, so he released the choke hold.

Joshua stood up. He cleared his throat, tightened his tie, and straightened his hat. Quinton went from one knee to sitting and slid to the corner of the elevator. He crossed his legs and placed his arms on his knees.

"So, what was that?" Quinton massaged his throat.

"One possible reality you could choose,"

"What happened to me?"

"Well, Quinton, your arrogance got you in trouble."

"What do you mean," Quinton asked and tilted his head.

"One evening, you were getting ready to leave work. You just got finished cheating on your wife with one of the new girls you hired. You were trying to make it home in time so you and your wife could go out for dinner. You had to keep up appearances, Quinton."

Quinton gave Joshua the middle finger.

"Then, before getting into your car, you decided to snort a few lines of coke and finish it off with seven shots of Jack. On your way home, someone pulled out in front of you and you rear-ended them. You were irate. You jumped out of the car in your drunken and doped up state, and without thinking, tried to pull the man from his car and teach him a lesson. Unfortunate for you, this man was gang member, and had three of his friends with him in the car. They beat you to a pulp, smashed the back of your neck with a bat. They shot you in the head and left you for dead. Oh, but Mr. Lucas, you were so fortunate. You did not die. Someone called 911 and help arrived in time. The bullet angle was just right ... or wrong, depending on your perspective. And loyal Cecilia? She took care of you, having no idea of what you had been doing to her."

"Enough Joshua! Enough!" Quinton put his hands over his ears and bared his teeth.

"Oh no, Quinton, I am not finished yet. You see, Quinton, your memory still functions, and cognitively, you are all there. But you can't talk, and you can't move. You just have to sit there, living with your guilt as you watch the woman you have been mistreating and cheating on for years express the depths of her loyalty to you by feeding you, wiping your butt, and bathing your fat body. But you? You can't say anything to her. You can't apologize; you can't be intimate with her again; nothing. And your kids?"

Joshua walked over to Quinton and leaned over him. "You get to watch them grow up before your eyes, without ever talking with them or interacting with them again. You will never get to apologize to them or get to spend quality time with them or tell them you love them. You are a spectator. Your wonderful life is right there in front of you, in your reach, yet you cannot enjoy it. How does that reality suit you, Mister Lucas?"

"No, no, no!" Quinton slammed both fist on the elevator floor and leaned his head back against the wall. His breathing picked up again. "What is this Joshua? Who are you?" Quinton now lifted his legs up, placing his head between his knees.

"This, Quinton Lucas, is justice; vengeance."

"What? Okay, so someone hates me … someone wants revenge for what I did to them, Big deal. Get over it," Quinton huffed.

"No, no, no, Quinton. You misunderstand. I said justice; vengeance, not revenge." Joshua stepped backwards.

"Don't play word games with me, asshole!" Quinton glared up at Joshua.

"It's not word games, Quinton, it is an important distinction."

"Revenge," stated Joshua as he paced around the elevator. "Revenge is punishing someone out of retaliation for a harm done. This is not retaliation. This is vengeance. Vengeance is simply punishment inflicted in return for the wrong done. It is not retaliation, it is justice. It is receiving the consequences for your actions. And you, Quinton, have come into the season of reaping. It is time for to you receive the reward for your actions."

"Says who!" Quinton popped his head up from between his knees.

"Says me."

"And who are you, God?"

Joshua paused then faced Quinton and smiled. "Now, Quinton, get at hold of yourself, you have some decisions to make." Joshua helped Quinton up and brushed his shoulders off.

"So, Quinton, is this the reality you want?"

"Wha … huh … no, no." Quinton coughed and massaged his throat again.

"Then choose another floor. You are wasting time. You have 45 minutes left."

"Uh … let's try down. Fourth floor, Joshua."

Joshua reached out and pushed the button for the fourth floor. The elevator began its decent. Quinton and Joshua stared at each other. The only sound was the hum of the elevator as it passed each floor. After a few awkward moments, the elevator stopped with a ding, and the doors opened.

Before them stood a metal rolling door to what looked like an abandoned warehouse.

"Are you ready to see what awaits you, Quinton," asked Joshua.

"Do I really have a choice?" Quinton placed his hands on his hips.

"Of course you do. You can choose another floor if you like."

"No, let's go in." Quinton took a deep breath, and the door of the warehouse opened.

Before them rested three metal folding chairs. In those chairs sat Quinton's wife and two children, tied with chains. Their mouths were duct taped, and in front of each of them was a stand. Bolted to each stand was a 12-gauge shotgun. The guns sat about three feet away and was aimed at their faces. Quinton's eyes bounced to his left, and he saw himself. In this reality, someone held him at gunpoint. It was a curly headed man with brown hair, and he wore tattered jeans and a blue flannel shirt.

"Oh dear … wha … what is this Joshua?" Quinton put his hands over his gaping mouth.

"This, my dear Quinton, is a former employee you screwed over. He worked in the warehouse of your dealership for fifteen years. He never missed a day of work, except for vacation. He was one of the best workers you had. But you wouldn't know, because you were too good to visit those, oh, what did you call them, 'vassals'?"

"Yeah, vassals." Quinton whispered as he stood stone-faced, eyes fixed on the mounted guns.

Joshua continued. "His name is Rick. He had a wife and four children he loved dearly. Rick could barely make ends meet. His wife soon developed cancer and died, and he was stuck with all these medical bills and raising his children on his own. He had no family either; no brother or sister. Parents on both his and his wife's side were dead. He came to you asking you for a raise. Remember?"

"Yeah, I do remember him." Quinton gave a slow nod.

"Do you remember what you told him," Joshua asked and cut his eyes at Quinton.

"No, not really." Quinto shrugged and broke his gaze away from the guns and gazed into Joshua's eyes. Those brown eyes; they resembled a sandstorm. Oh, how Quinton wanted to rip them out and stomp the shit out of them till they splattered all over the elevator.

"Well, let me refresh your memory, Quinton." Joshua motioned with his arm towards the open doors. He and Quinton returned their gaze to the unfolding drama. "Now, Rick has never received a raise, mind you. Not in fifteen years. When he told you his story and asked you for mercy, do you know what you did? Do you remember?"

See ELEVATOR, page 34

ELEVATOR, cont. from page 33

Quinton shook his head.

"You told him 'no', Quinton. And that is not the worst of it. He came back several times over the next few days begging you. And you know what you did then, Quinton? You fired him!" Joshua banged the back of his fist against the wall of the elevator.

Quinton flinched.

"That's right," Joshua composed himself. "You fired him. You told him you were tired of his moaning and complaining, so you fired him."

A flash or remembrance lit Quinton's face, and he snickered "Yeah, I remember him. What a shmuck. But he didn't do this, Joshua. He just walked out the door and left. I never heard from him again."

"Right Quinton, in your world he did, but this is a different reality. In this reality, Rick seeks vengeance. Your harshness and merciless acts send him over the edge. He snaps. So, he drags you, your wife, and your kids down to this warehouse one night to dish out justice. Here's the deal, Quinton. Rick is a smart man; a mechanical genius. He has those shotguns connected and synced to all go off at the same time."

"So," Quinton shrugged. "He's going to kill my family all at once and make me watch?" Quinton studied the horror on the faces of his wife and children. The arrogance deflated from Quinton's face.

"No, Quinton, it is much worse," Joshua said.

"What could be worse than that?" Anger replaced arrogance.

"You have to choose which one you are going to save. You see Quinton, all three of those guns are rigged to go off at the same time, and you are going to have to choose who you will save by stepping in front of the gun. If you do not choose a family member to save, then Rick is going to shoot you. Either way, you die. And if you do not make a choice, everybody dies. Who are you going to save Quinton?" Joshua placed an arm around Quinton and pointed. "The wife you cheated on or one of the children you neglected? You can only save one."

"No! No! No!" Quinton jerked away from Joshua "This is sick! Who the hell comes up with this shit? Who comes up with this so-called reality?! Enough of this crap." Quinton tried to leap through the elevator towards Rick. He smacked into an invisible force and flew back against the back of the elevator.

"Ugh … whaa …?" Quinton rubbed his balding head.

"That's not going to work, Quinton. These are images. These realities will not take form for you until you decide on which one you will choose. If you keep this up, the only thing you will succeed in doing his hurting yourself."

Joshua walked over to Quinton and helped him off the floor. Quinton wheezed and hacked out a few loud coughs. "This is bull—"

"No, Quinton, it is reaping what you sow."

Quinton stared at Joshua again. He took a few deep breaths, and then it hit him. The unsettling realization that the only way out was to choose. "Please, Joshua," Quinton began to tear up, and a look of exhaustion filled his face, "get me out of here."

"So, I am guessing you do not want this reality."

"No, please, I can't take it. Another floor, please."

"As you wish." Joshua helped Quinton back into the elevator. The doors shut, and Joshua spoke. "Quinton, if you try a stunt like that again, I am going to assume you have made your decision. Step off the elevator again, and your fate is final. Do you understand?".

Quinton started to take rasping breaths, "Why?! Why?! Why?! Why are you doing this Joshua?"

"Do you understand?!"

"Yes, yes, yes. Won't happen again. But why? Why all this?"

"It has already been explained to you Quinton. I am not going to repeat myself. However, what you do need to know is all these realities have one thing in common."

Quinton motioned at Joshua with his hands, beckoning him to continue.

"They are a far cry from what you had before. None of these realities will be pleasant. They will include hardship, tragedy, and loss. Life will never be the same for you, Quinton."

"I don't want to play anymore, do you hear me! No more! Not me! I don't want to play!" Quinton banged the elevator walls. Sanity fled from his body. He lifted his hands and faced the camera. "Not me everybody! Not me!"

"Quinton, this is not a game. You have had your fun. You have wasted your life and did not appreciate everything given to you." Joshua stood calm and collected, as Quinton gave his best Jack Torrance.

"C'mon Joshua, there has to be something else … something else … some …" Quinton fell back again into the corner of the elevator and slid down, head between his legs. "Some other way."

"Yes, there is one more thing." Joshua said, holding up his pointer finger. "All of these alternate realities parallel your life and will end in death. All but one, that is. And this one … Well, let's just say you will be trapped in one reoccurring event for all eternity. I know, not the words you were hoping for, but it is different."

Joshua patted Quinton on the shoulder. Quinton looked at Joshua and cursed him for about thirty seconds. Joshua shook his head in disbelief.

"You see, Quinton. This is exactly your problem. Instead of being remorseful over all you have done, you continue in your pride and arrogance. You sit here and cry and sob, not because you are sorry for the things you have done, but because you are now inconvenienced. You are sorry you got caught, sorry what you have is being taken from you. Your repentance is not repentance. It is self-pity."

Quinton sat there, with his head still between his legs, taking in deep breaths, ignoring Joshua's babble.

"Get up, Quinton. You have thirty minutes left. Which floor, sir?"

Quinton grabbed the handicap railing in the elevator and pulled himself up. He wiped his face with his hands, let out a deep breath, and said, "Thirteen, lucky thirteen. Why not? We are in a casino, right?"

Joshua reached out and pushed the 13th floor button, "Nice to see you are having a sense of humor about this Quinton. But what awaits you on the thirteenth floor—I don't think you will find very humorous."

The elevator made its familiar hum, as it climbed to the 13th floor. Those moments seemed to Quinton to hang in the air and dissipate slower than the morning fog he would see at his home in Castle Rock. The elevator stopped, and the familiar ding rang out.

"Here we are Quinton, lucky thirteen," Joshua said, with an air of sarcasm in his voice.

As the doors opened, Quinton noticed the mirrors. He saw himself sitting on the floor, wearing a one-piece jump suit, brownish in color.

"What is this?" Quinton glanced at Joshua, but Joshua's eyes stayed fixed on the room.

"Notice the room, Quinton. It is perfectly round, with a dome roof. The circumference is eight feet. The room is all mirrors; no windows, no doors. No way in; no way out."

"How do you know this, Joshua?"

"I designed it, Quinton."

"Wha …"

"It is a room designed to drive you insane." Joshua smiled, his face exuberant with the satisfaction of an artist who has created a masterpiece. "Look at yourself Quinton. That is what I want you to do. Look at yourself. See who you really are. Stare at yourself from all angles. No matter how hard you try, you cannot get away from who you really are."

Joshua now turned and faced Quinton.

"Quinton, you fill your life with pleasure, because you cannot stand yourself. This is ironic, since in a way, you worship yourself. You have made an idol of yourself and your pleasure, because you think if you fill your life with these things, you will finally be able to accept yourself and find fulfillment. But this is not true … it simply is not true."

"Joshua," Quinton lifted his head. "You're insane. You're the crazy one, not me! What kind of person designs these sorts of things?! What type of person thinks this up?! What sort of person does this?!"

"A person charged with the duty of dealing out vengeance, Quinton."

"Well, Joshua, this isn't vengeance, it is torture. It is sadistic!"

"From your limited, distorted point of view it may seem that way. Let me explain. It doesn't seem fair to you because you are on the receiving end. But oh, to all those you have harmed, from their perspective, it is fair. You are getting what you deserve."

Quinton turned his gaze away from Joshua and back to the room of mirrors. Knowing by now that arguing got him nowhere, Quinton asked, "So, Joshua, enlighten me more about this room."

"Well, Quinton, there is not much to tell. You have been taken away from your family. Now, all you have is the memories of what you have done to them. You do not know how you got here, and you do not know why you are here."

"Well, can't you tell me?"

"No, because if I did, then it would change the reality that has been planned for this floor. In this reality, you are to have no memory of why or how."

"This is …"

"This is what, Quinton?"

"Nothing."

"Quinton, I have already told you about the mirrors, but I will proceed further. You are left here with your memories and yourself. You can scream all you want, but no one will hear you because there is no one to hear you. You are alone; isolated. All you have is yourself, Quinton. You cannot run anymore. You must face yourself and your sin. Look at who you are. Look at what you have become."

Quinton began to pace back in forth in the elevator again, anger filling him again like hot poison. He kicked the elevator wall behind them and banged his fist like a toddler throwing a temper tantrum.

"Who do you think you are, Joshua?! How dare you stand in judgment of me! You sit there with that pious look on your face. Who or what gives you the right?!

Spit flew everywhere, and his thinning hair danced into shambles. Quinton's body quaked as various emotions jockeyed for dominance. Joshua, not moved at all by Quinton's childish fit, took off his hat,

See ELEVATOR, page 36

ELEVATOR, cont. from page 35

held it in both hands, and watched Quinton unravel.

"I do not have to explain myself to you Quinton. Deep down, you know who I am, and you know why I have the power to do this. Now, Quinton, do you want this floor for your reality? Make a choice, you have 17 minutes left."

"No … no … not this one. Definitely not this one. This is the last one I would choose."

"Very well, sir. Where to next?" Joshua put his hat back on, and awaited Quinton's response.

"Uh … let's go back down. First floor, Joshua."

Joshua reached over and pushed the button for the first floor.

"You know what Joshua? You are gonna pay for what you're doing. You know that? One day you are gonna get what you deserve, you self-righteous pig." Quinton wiped his forehead with his sleeve.

"Mr. Lucas, you still don't get it do you? Are you still so slow to understand? This is not about me, but about you. You need to stop trying to blame me for your problems. You have brought this on yourself."

Quinton got nose to nose with Joshua. "Stop talking in riddles to me, Joshua! Speak plainly!"

Joshua, unmoved by Quinton's threatening gesture, answered, "I have spoken plainly to you all your life, but you refused to listen."

Quinton's mind staggered. He knew. He knew who Joshua was, and fear now dug into the marrow of his bones. Before Quinton could respond, the elevator stopped, and the doors opened. There before them laid two hospital beds. Quinton recognized the hospital—the Presbyterian hospital where his two children were born.

As Quinton and Joshua drew closer, Quinton got a good look at who rested in the beds. When he did, his color left him, and Joshua had to grab him before he fell to the floor. There in the two beds, lay two figures who somewhat resembled his wife and him. They stared into each other's eyes, taking long, hard breaths. Tubes and wires protruded from each of them, and monitors in the back ground beeped at a steady pace.

"What happened, Joshua?" Quinton asked, dazed, with one arm around Joshua for support.

"Well, Quinton, both you and your wife are sick and dying."

"Why?" By this time, Quinton didn't know why he asked, because he didn't even want to know.

"You both have AIDS."

Quinton let go of Joshua and fell to his knees. As Quinton sobbed, Joshua placed one hand on his shoulder and continued.

"Quinton, in this reality, your promiscuous lifestyle does not end well. Not for anyone. In this reality, you contracted AIDS from one of the many women you slept with. Then, you spread it to your wife. But not only your wife Quinton, to many other women also. The horrible thing about this entire situation is you knew you had the disease. But you were so selfish, you didn't care who you spread it to. Instead of causing you to stop messing around, out of anger you wanted to make as many people suffer right along with you. Even your faithful and devoted wife. That is what she gets for sticking with you Quinton; for being loyal to you. She gets AIDS. She gets death."

"My children, where are my children Joshua?" The fight left Quinton, and his voice rasped a dry whisper.

"Well, all those women you intentionally infected? They sued you, and you pleaded guilty. Everything was taken from you, and because of both your, and Cecilia's, condition your children were taken from you and put into foster care. You single handedly screwed over your family. Now, you have to lie there, staring into the eyes of the wife you murdered. She gave you loyalty, and you gave her AIDS."

"I … I didn't murder her."

"Oh, Mister Lucas, you did. You most certainly did. You knew you had the disease, and you refused to tell her. You are the sole cause of her death. Now, you have to watch her die. Her blood is on your hands. How does it feel, Quinton?"

"No, Joshua … I can't take it anymore. Shut the door. Shut the door!" Quinton's cries of torment echoed in his own ears. His voice sounded foreign to him, like someone he never met.

"So, this reality doesn't suit you, Quinton?"

Quinton turned his back to the scene and walked toward the corner of the elevator.

"I take that as a no, Quinton. Where to next? You have six minutes."

Upon hearing this news, Quinton slipped from sorrowful to apeshit. He whipped around towards Joshua and hollered, "Six minutes! Six minutes! I am not playing your game anymore, Joshua! I'm done! I'm gonna kill you! Let me off this elevator now!"

"You can get off anytime you wish, Quinton. Just pick a floor, and I will let you off."

"I hate you Joshua! I hate this elevator! You are driving me insane! This elevator is driving me insane! This isn't fair! Not fair, Joshua! Not fair! How am I to make a decision when I don't have time to visit every floor! This is rigged in order to screw me over!"

Joshua let Quinton finish his rant before he responded, "Fair, Quinton? Do you want to hear about fair? It wasn't fair to your wife for you to cheat on her all these years. It wasn't fair for your children to go neglected all these years. It wasn't fair to Rick for you to fire him. It wasn't fair for all those people you cheated out of money. It's not fair for you to cheat on your taxes. Need I go on Quinton? Life is not fair, but justice is. You have two minutes to make a decision, or one will be made for you."

Quinton banged his head against the elevator. His maddening laugh proof he had crossed over to the land of the insane. "Oh, Joshua, Joshua, Joshua. You are quite the puppeteer. What, do you enjoy this stuff? Is this how you get your kicks?"

Joshua took in a deep breath and let out a heavy sigh, "No, Quinton, I don't enjoy seeing people suffer. Even wicked people like you. I don't enjoy what I do, but it must be done. I would rather see people turn from their wicked ways. However, when they don't, they must face the consequences of their actions. You have one minute remaining."

Quinton perused the buttons. He wondered what horror lay behind each floor. Could they be worse than what he has already seen? Maybe. Probably. But one thing he was sure of—he was not going to let Joshua pick for him. Joshua would surely give him the shaft.

"Thirty seconds, Mr. Lucas."

Quinton winced.

"Twenty seconds."

Which floor! Which floor! Not 1, not 4, not 13.

"Ten seconds."

Pick Quinton, pick! Hurry!

"Five seconds."

Quinton made up his mind. "Twenty-five!" he blurted out. "I want floor twenty-five."

"The top floor, Mr. Lucas? Very well."

Joshua reached out his hand and pushed the button for the 25 floor. Quinton's chest felt heavy. His vision blurred. He tried to swallow but couldn't. He had to gain his composure. Had to get the last word. He needed to let Joshua know he figured it out. Before they reached the top floor, Quinton spoke. "Well, Joshua, one thing I was sure of is I was not going to let you pick for me. And besides, I already discovered the room with the one reoccurring event."

"Oh, you did?" Joshua raised his eyebrow.

"Yes, I did. It was the room with the mirrors. That was it. I figured it out. One room with no way in or out. Not knowing how I got there or why. Left to look at myself in those wretched mirrors for all eternity; oh yeah, I figured it out Joshua. I figured it out, and I figured you out. That is just the thing you would love to do to me. To see me in that room for all eternity."

Joshua let out a boisterous laugh, head tilted back and mouth gaping. "Oh, Mr. Lucas, I am afraid you are dead wrong. You would have died in that room in less than a week due to starvation and dehydration. Actually, the room you speak of was the most lenient of all the others. It seems what you have tried to avoid has now become your fate. The events of floor twenty-five will repeat for all eternity."

Fear and terror made their way into Quinton like slithering serpents. All the color left his face, and he dry heaved. The elevator bell dinged, and the doors opened. "No, Joshua! No! No!" Quinton ran and clung to Joshua, with a look of horror on his face. Tears filled Quinton's eyes, and he bawled. "Don't make me go! Don't make me go!"

"You have made your choice, Quinton. Your time is up."

Joshua freed himself from Quinton and moved him out of the elevator with a gentle push. Quinton, still facing Joshua, with his back towards his new reality, made sure Joshua heard just one more time how Quinton felt about him.

"I hate you, Joshua! I hate you, you know that! At least I won't have to see you anymore, you jack ass." Quinton flipped him off.

The doors of the elevator shut, and Quinton banged on them, continuing to curse Joshua. After he composed himself, he turned around to meet his fate.

"Welcome to the Grand Casino and Hotel, Mr. Lucas, glad you will be staying with us again," the man behind the front desk said. His frame was tall and lanky, and he wore a blue blazer and khaki pants.

What?! What is this?! No, turn around and run! Turn around and run out the door, Quinton.

But Quinton couldn't do that, he could only walk towards the front desk

"Thanks, Raul, always good to see you."

No, it's not good to see you! Get me out of here! Raul! Help me!

"Mister Lucas, if you would, please follow Joshua. He will take your bags and get you on the elevator."

Oh dear God, no! Not Joshua! He's insane, Raul! Do you know that?! Do you know you have a madman working for you?! I will not follow him

No matter how hard Quinton fought it in his head, he couldn't do anything different.

"Joshua? What happened to the smokin' hot girl you had … oh,

See ELEVATOR, page 38

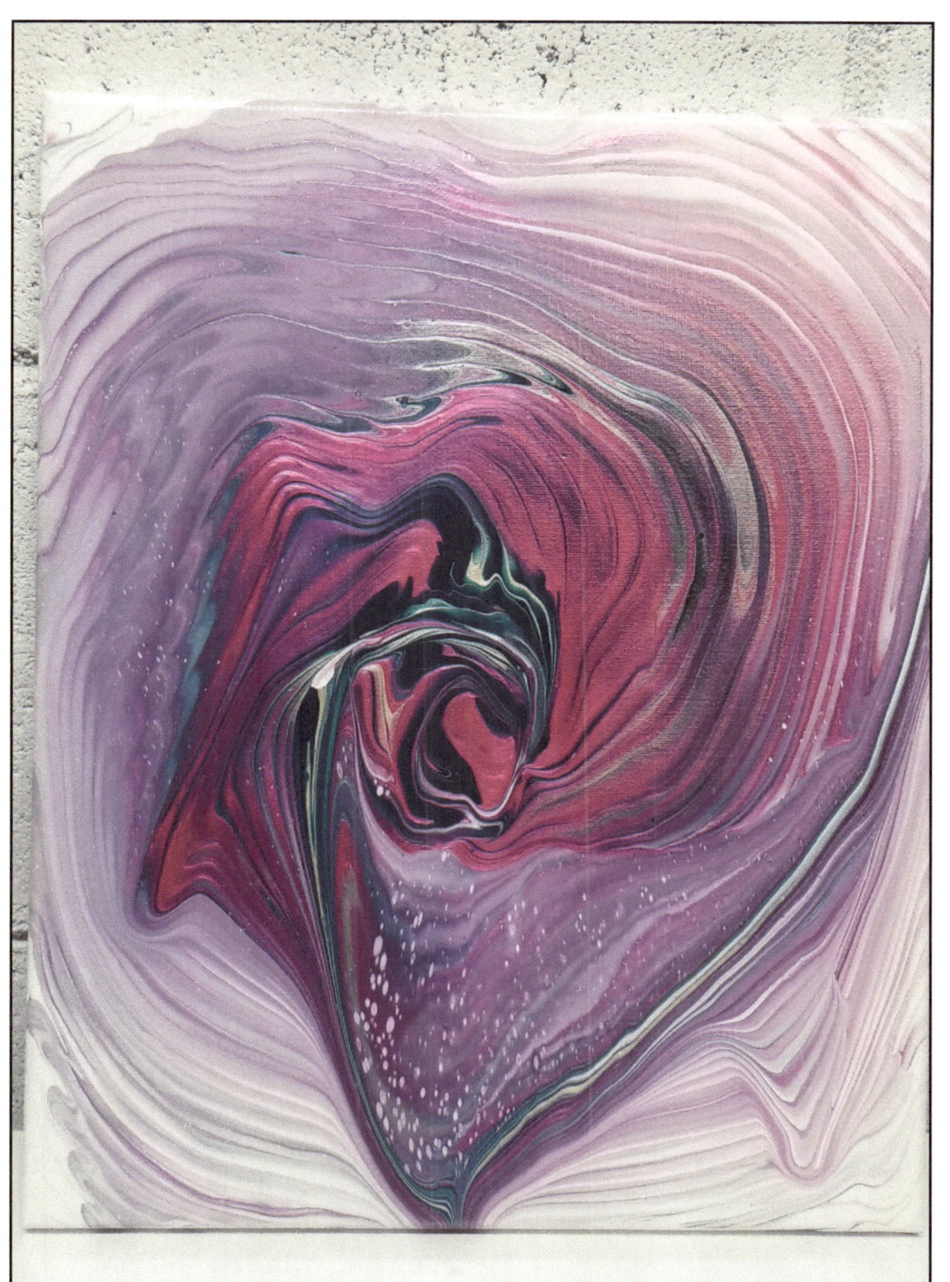

Controlled Cha-os on Canvas

by Cate Brown (left) and Logan Brown (right)

You can find more of Cate's and Logan's work on Facebook at Cate's Chaotic Creations.

https://www.facebook.com/Cates-Chaot-ic-Creations-113445590484536

"Double, double toil and trouble; fire burn and cauldron bubble."

Macbeth (William Shakespeare)

ELEVATOR, cont. from page 37

what was her name … oh yeah, Sophia?" Quinton raised a bushy eye-brow.

"I'm sorry, Mr. Lucas," Raul said. "We had to let her go last week. It seems her extra- curricular activities were carrying over into her job."

A mistake, Raul! A mistake! What were you thinking?!

"What does that mean, Raul?"

"Take it to mean whatever you wish, Mr. Lucas." Raul grinned and rapped his fingers on the desk.

Quinton snickered. Then turned and followed Joshua onto the elevator.

No, no, no …

"Joshua, huh?" Quinton folded his arms and scowled.

"Yes sir, at your service." Joshua bowed.

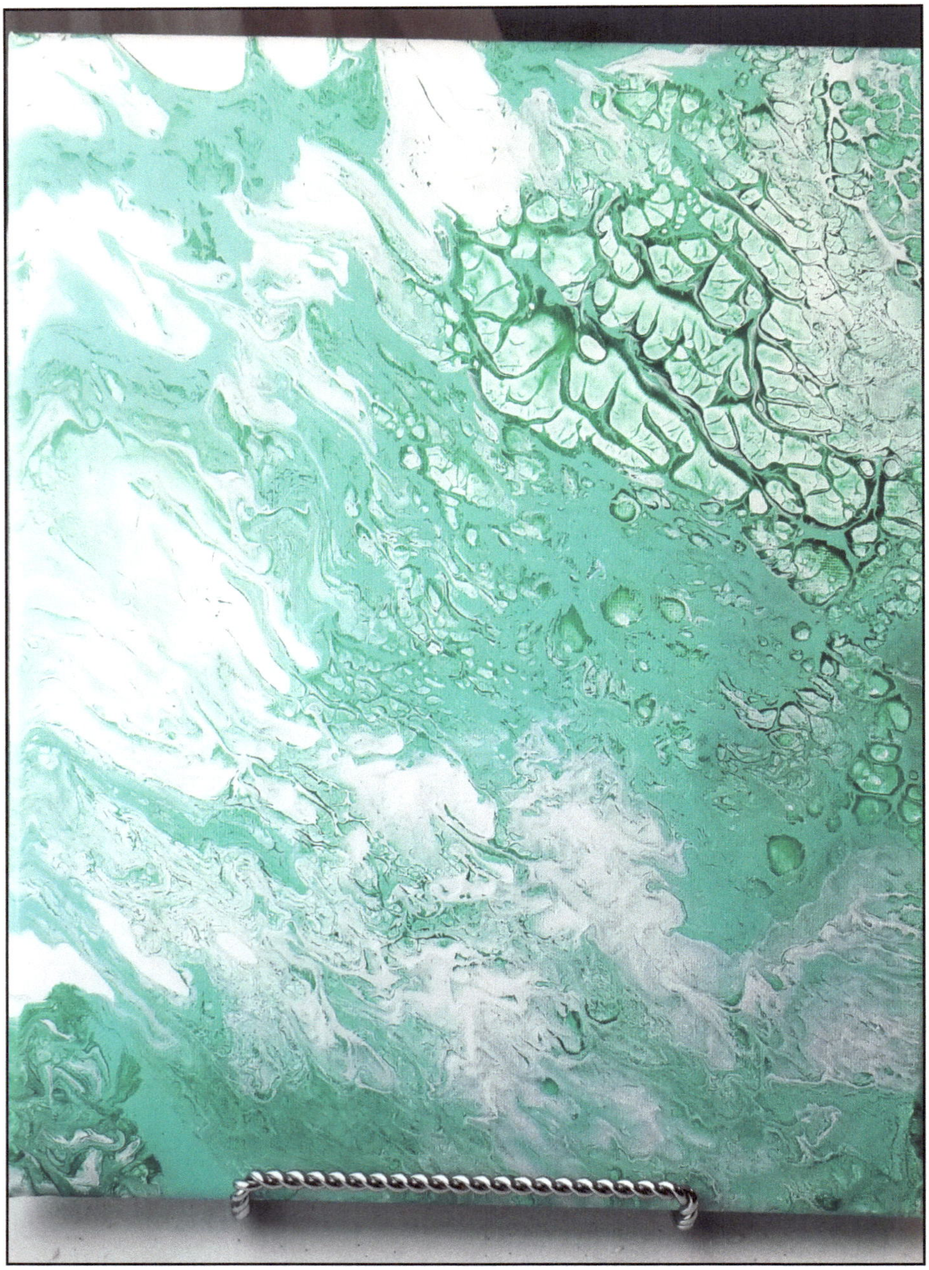

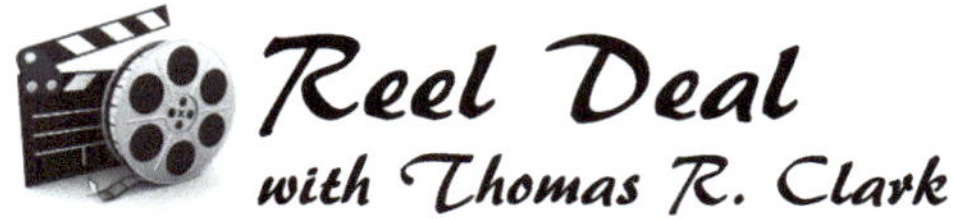

Can AMC tap a new vein with The Vampire Chronicles?

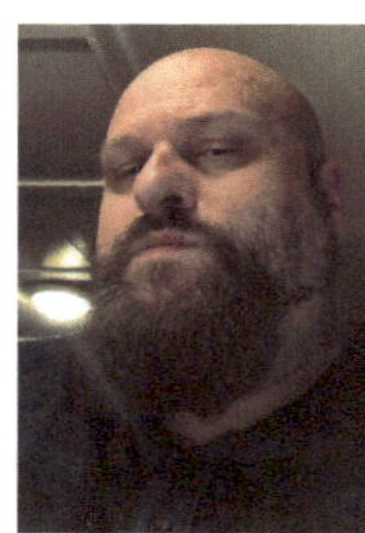

Zombies are dead.

Literally.

After two decades of having them shoved down our collective throats, the writing is scrawled on the wall in caked blood. Much like a dying body, the zombie trope kicks and thrashes as it dies, occasionally landing a solid blow. But they're getting weaker and further apart. A time will come when the zombie is no longer the darling of horror fiction on the page or screen. Sure, you get the occasional Train To Busan, which reinvigorates the subgenre for a time. Most small presses avoid zombie themed books now. The mainstream zombie title, The Walking Dead, has seen a slip in viewership since series lead Andrew Lincoln departed. The comic book also saw the end of its run, most recently, with 193 issues in the bank.

In spite of this decline, AMC, The Walking Dead's television partner, is tripling down on the show's success with a pair of spin-offs and theatrical feature plans. They've seen how lucrative the horror genre is with well produced programming. The most recent entry being an adaptation of Dan Simmons' The Terror. Smart executives at the network know The Walking Dead won't last forever. They want to keep the audience they've grown from cable going into this streaming age.

Enter Anne Rice.

May 2020 brought the announcement the long time writer of things gothic and creepy, signed a deal with AMC for the production rights to her immense library known as The Vampire Chronicles and the Mayfair Witches. Starting with Interview With The Vampire, the series has lasted for decades and includes a pair of theatrical adaptations. One is beloved, the other not so much. But the time is ripe for a new interpretation of Rice's influential undead classics.

Vampires are in a resurgence. They have a longer track record of success, overall, than zombies could ever achieve. BBC's Dracula reimagining broke streaming records and a Lost Boys series in development at the CW Network. The

See CHRONICLES, page 40

CHRONICLES, cont. from page 39

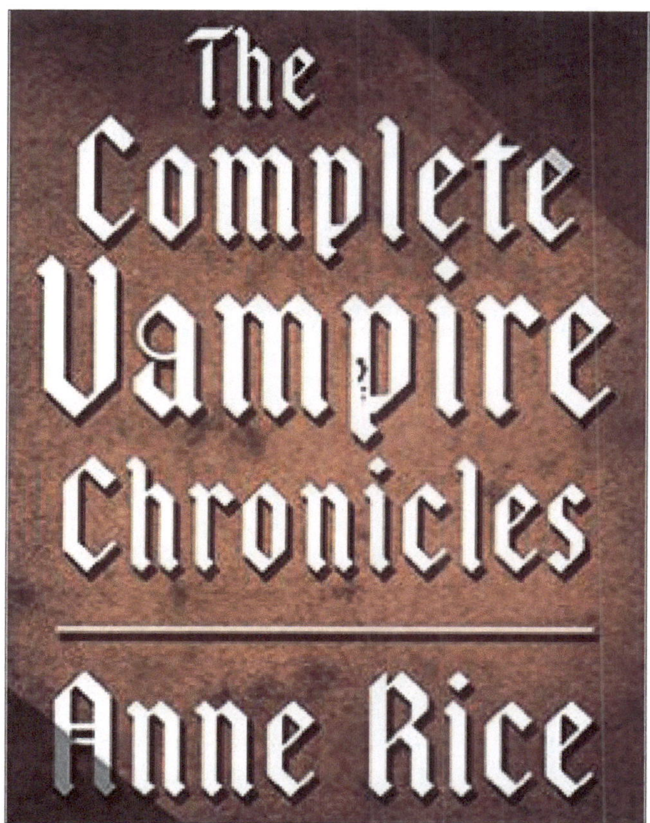

popularity of FX's What We Do In The Shadows, along with Twilight scribe Stephanie Myers returning to her world, are indicators the prince and princesses of the night aren't going away anytime soon. In fact, they're rising in the dark to feast on your wallet. Marvel's announcements of bringing vampire hunter Blade into the MCU, as well as SONY's Morbius The Living Vampire, is another clear indicator the public wants more blood sucking freaks.

Yes, vampires once again rule the night.

The Vampire Chronicles focuses on the legendary prince of vampires, Lestat de Lioncourt. First introduced in Interview With The Vampire as the story's antagonist, Rice flipped the trope on its head by returning to tell Lestat's story in her follow up, the best selling The Vampire Lestat. Instead of the villain, he became the hero. She wrapped up this trilogy with Queen Of The Damned. Then Anne moved on to tell stories about the Mayfair Witches in gigantic volumes that double as doorstops. More vampire books followed at a slower pace, coming out every three or four years until she tied them all together in Merrick in 2000, culminating with Blood Canticle in 2003. In total eighteen novels between the Vampires and Witches of Anne Rice's muse.

And Rice was done with it. Blood Canticle was the last story to tell.

A few years earlier, the longtime atheist literally rediscovered God. She returned to Catholicism in 1998, and after Blood Canticle, wrote about Jesus for a few books. This lasted until 2014's Prince Lestat. Rice hasn't left the vampire world she created since, flushing out and completing the story of her beloved vampire hero, Lestat. These additional volumes make for twenty-one stories. It's a wealth of entertainment for decades to come. And AMC has them at their disposal. Anne's son, Christopher Rice, is heavily involved with the projects (he's rumored to ghost write for his mother), including screenplay adaptations of his mother's works. This is a good sign the stories will stay true to Rice's gothic vision on the screen in all their blood, guts and gayness.

The Vampire Chronicles can only be described as sexy, deviant, and violent … all dipped in copious buckets of blood. Fans of Bryan Fuller's Hannibal may have caught a glimpse into the societal taboos we will witness on the screen in this series. But what a difference almost a decade makes. Like Hannibal's bromance between Will and Lector, there is no doubt the stories are gay. But in this modern era of open acceptance, Anne Rice's vampires might be the LGBTQ Community's dark heroes.

I won't postulate on casting. There are so many young, hungry actors out there, I want a cast of unknowns with an occasional face we might recognize. No names, like they did with The Walking Dead. Really, outside of Norman Reedus and Michael Rooker it was a bunch of nobodies with talent and a great showrunner in Frank Darabont (and later Greg Nicotero). As news breaks on the talent involved, both on the screen and behind the scenes, we'll get a better idea of the show and in what direction it will go.

Still, the question remains, are Rice's vampires the secret to AMC's long lasting success in the new age of streaming? Are they a literal vein to tap in a money mine? Or dare I say the necks of viewers? Will blood pour gold into AMC's coffers? I'll reserve passing any judgment now. We won't know if they nail it or not until the product airs. All of the markers for success are there. Now all that remains to be seen is can they pull it off?

Or will the sun rise prematurely on this vampire resurgence?

Music Notes
with Peter Molnar

Marilyn Manson still delivers the music

"Heaven Upside Down" by Marilyn Manson (2017)

When Marilyn Manson buzz sawed their way onto the charts with their first single "Get Your Gunn" from their debut album *Portrait of an American Family* (1994), the music world was still enamored by the Grunge movement. Bands like Nirvana, Pearl Jam, and Alice in Chains reigned supreme with their downer rock and slow, burning guitar riffs that harkened back to the likes of Black Sabbath and mid-70s Led Zeppelin. Whereas Grunge encouraged Generation X to swallow the bitter pill over and over, Marilyn Manson's insanely aggressive, occult-laced metal and their over-the-top live creepshows rammed that pill down your throat, held your mouth closed, and bashed you over the head a couple of times to ensure compliance. Manson, the band's ringleader and unapologetic "God of Fuck", has always prided himself on titillation of the masses and a steady, thrumming, and consistent provocation of the holier-than-thou. The sacred is defamed in his lyrics, and the notorious uplifted in equal measure.

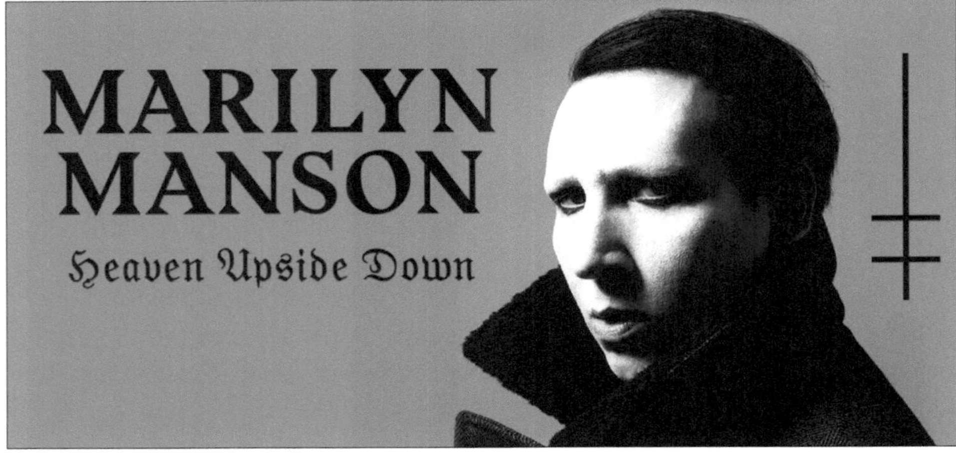

Just to give you some idea of what a Manson show is like, I went to see them at The Electric Factory in Philadelphia for their *Holywood* tour. I had heard so much about the band's already legendary stage show, complete with pyrotechnics from Hell, Manson on stilts, and the ghoulishly unsettling appearances of the bandmembers in their strange wigs and bizarre makeup. I'd heard Manson frequently cut himself on stage and berated the audience, much to their twisted delight. The "threat" of what could happen at a Marilyn Manson show was what made it and the band so thrilling and different and exciting all at once. That night in Philly, the dread was palpable! There was no promise of safety at a Marilyn Manson show, and in equal measure, there is no such promise in any of Marilyn Manson's music. Not since the days of Iggy Pop and GG Allin has a band's unsafe, malignant reputation divided audiophiles into the fiercely loyal and the utterly appalled.

Fast forward twenty-three years. By 2017, the band has gone through frequent and extensive line-up changes. Their sound had inevitably undergone a series of changes as well. Their sophomore effort, arguably their best, *Antichrist Superstar,* witnessed the band at its heaviest and most brilliant with its over-arcing "storyline from Hell" and such gut-punching tracks as "The Beautiful People" and "Reflecting God". From there, Marilyn Manson delved into such genres as Glam Rock (*Mechanical Animals,* 1998), industrial (*The Golden Age of Grotesque*, 2003), lo-fi metal (*Born Villain*, 2012), and, perhaps most surprising and inventive of all, blues rock (*The Pale Emperor*, 2015). With their latest effort, *Heaven Upside Down,* the band's tenth studio album, Marilyn Manson sounds like a band that has come full circle in its sonic experimentation. *Heaven* carries the varied, stylistic residue of the band's entire discography in its ten tracks.

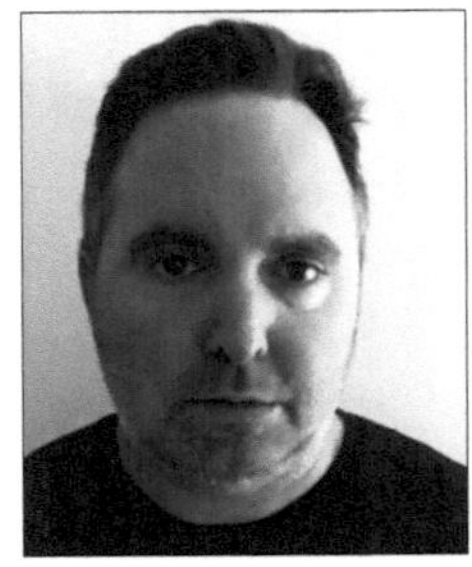

The good news? The threat of Marilyn Manson is alive and well so many years later.

Heaven Upside Down (Hell, etc. Records) resembles its critically acclaimed predecessor, *The Pale Emperor*, due in part to the absence of Manson's songwriting partner, Twiggy Ramirez, who was unavailable for both albums due to scheduling conflicts, as well as a legal battle the bassist had become embroiled in involving an alleged sexual assault in 1990. Ramirez was one of the band's co-founders, and he and Manson had separated for six years before regrouping for the band's seventh album, *The High End of Low.* Ramirez's absence is obvious,

See MANSON, page 42

"Tell me what thy lordly name is on the Night's Plutonian shore!
Quoth the Raven, 'Nevermore.'"
THE RAVEN (Edgar Allan Poe)

MANSON, cont. from page 41

and not just because the tracks lack his signature booming fuzz-box bass. The Manson-Ramirez writing team had produced some of the finest work to come out of the band's extensive discography, and the macabre sound and stage performance was fostered in large part by the now absent bassist and songwriter. A great deal of that spook factor has been lost, but the music still has teeth.

Marilyn Manson's current producer, Tyler Bates, is no doubt a godsend to what many view as the band's second act. Manson has found in Bates a new writing partner who is every bit as in tune with what makes the band's music signature and downright unsettling in its delivery as Twiggy Ramirez was. The two met through mutual involvement in the Showtime series *Californication*. This was a marriage made in Hell, no doubt. Bates is a film composer with many noteworthy credits to his name, such as Rob Zombie's *The Devil's Rejects* and *Guardians of the Galaxy,* as well as tv scores for shows like *Bates Motel*. He teamed up with Manson for *The Pale Emperor*, and it is no accident that album would prove a risky but masterful departure from what the band had been doing up until 2015. This is because even the blues-rock album by Marilyn Manson still managed to retain the menace fans have come to love and expect from the band.

"Revelation #12", the first track on *Heaven Upside Down,* hearkens back to the heavy-metal mayhem and screeching, overly provocative lyrics of *Superstars* live opener "Irresponsible Hate Anthem". Manson sounds like the "Reverend" he used to be, preaching from the pulpit of fire and damnation like some Old Testament prophet. He questions the origins of evil in man when he asks, "Is it the Devil or us?" There is also the fact he sounds as vitriolic and rage filled as ever, which is no small feat decades on. Manson screams the track like his own feet are being held to the very fire he preaches of. Another high point of the album is its first single, "We Know Where You Fucking Live", released on September 11, 2017. The theme of "evil's origin" has begun to take shape by this third track, and compounds Manson's indictment of human cruelty as separate of what is a beautiful planet and a mythical Satan. He asks, "What's a nice place like this, doing round people like us?" The lyrics are violent and primal and the lyrical equivalent of a home invasion. "Kill4Me", the second single, became the group's highest charting song on Billboard's Mainstream Rock. It is a strangely danceable number, which breaks the crushing forward momentum leading up to it. "Say10", which was the original working title for the album, delves into the brooding, creeping sinister thought process of the front man, backed by its low, lurching industrial beat that builds into a growling chorus crescendo. Its lyrics are unmistakably autobiographical, a rarity for much of the Manson catalog. He seems to lament something lost, perhaps the vitality the stage used to offer him and no longer does: "Something is shedding its skin/Crying from the heat of the light/Or the empty shell on the stage/And cash is a poor man's money". The epic, galloping "Saturnalia" wants to build to a grand finale, but it never reaches such heights and runs on until it quite simply runs out of juice. The song is a low point that is quickly redeemed by tracks like "Jesus Crisis" and the thrashing final track, "Threats of Romance" which rounds out the album in a neat soul-crushing fashion. The ever hopeless, and sadistic Manson makes no apologies for his cold heart in the end song: "I like you damaged, but I need something left/Something for me, something for me to wreck".

Manson has recently begun teasing a new album in the coming months. The latest tweet was in Latin and translates to "All deaf and now you hear me", with hashtags like #everyonewillsuffernow and #2020 and #youhavenoideawhatiscoming. With the way the band's music has been evolving of late, one can only assume and hope their upward trajectory continues. After all, somebody's got to save rock n' roll, eh?

Rating: 9/10

Bran Castle captures imagination of vampire fans

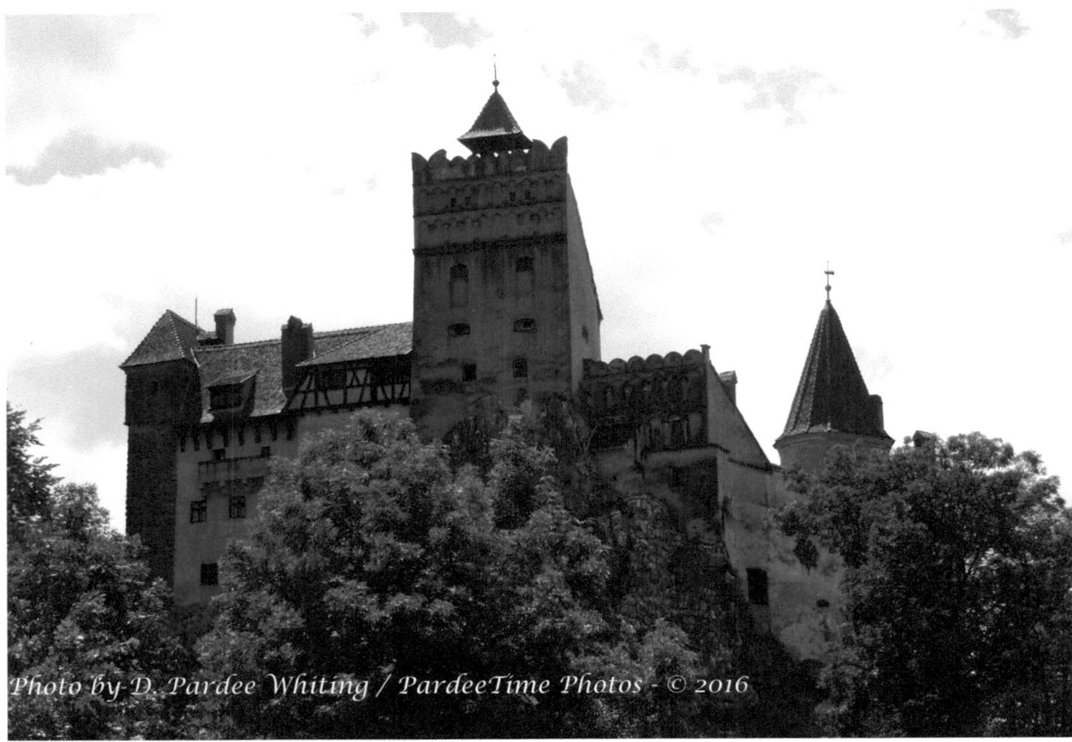

Bran Castle - Transylvania, Romania.

By D. Pardee Whiting

Just as stories capture our imagination, so do the places where they take place, such as the Bermuda Triangle and Roswell, New Mexico. However, one place that will always hold a horror fan's fascination is Bran Castle, affectionately known in vampire lore as Dracula's Castle.

Most horror fans, if not all, are familiar with Bram Stoker's 1897 novel Dracula and how the titular character, a vampire, lived in a castle nestled in a mountain pass in the Carpathian Mountains.

While scholars believe Stoker drew inspiration for the famed vampire Count Dracula from Romanian folklore about the nosferatu—the undead who rise at night to prey on the living—it is also widely accepted the Irish born author based his vampire on the 15th century Romanian prince, Vlad Țepeș.

Țepeș was the second son of nobleman Vlad II Dracul (Romanian for Dragon) and would serve as voivode (local ruler/governor) of Wallachia three separate times between 1448 and his death in 1477 while the territory was under Hungarian rule. According to historians, he took the surname Dracula (Romanian for son of Dracul) when he was initiated, like his father before him, into the secret order of Christian knights known as the Order of the Dragon.

As the ruler of Wallachia, which is now part of Romania, Țepeș was known for his brutality against anyone he considered as enemies. Țepeș (Romanian for the Impaler) willingly employed torture, mutilation, mass murder, disembowelment, decapitation, and boiling or skinning his victims alive. However, his preferred method is reported to be impalement—driving a sharpened wooden stake through his victim's bodies—and leaving them to die.

During his campaign against the Ottoman invaders in 1462, Țepeș is known to have left up to 20,000 victims impaled along the banks of the Danube River. Some gruesome accounts claim Țepeș liked to dine among the impaled bodies of his victims and dip his bread in their blood.

The consensus among scholars is it is these details, in addition to Țepeș' legally adopted name of Dracula and his birthplace in Transylvania, that cemented the creation of Count Dracula in Stoker's book.

As for the setting of the bloodsucker's home, Castle Dracula, many believe it to be modeled after Bran Castle despite Vlad Țepeș never having lived there. However, he is known to have passed through the Bran Gorge several times during his campaigns, and at one point attacked and looted the area following a dispute with the traders living there.

Before the stone castle was built in the mountain pass, there was a wooden fortress built by the Knights of the Teutonic Order in 1212, which was later destroyed by the Mongols in 1242.

In 1377, permission to build the stone castle, later known as Bran Castle, was granted to the Saxons of Kronstadt in an effort to better protect a trade route through the Southern Carpathian Mountains. The only condition was the construction was to be at the Saxons' expense and labor. During this time the settlement of Bran began to develop.

Throughout its early history, the castle was also used for defense against the Ottoman Empire, and later became a customs post on the mountain pass between Wallachia and Transylvania. Most castles during that time belong to nobility; however, historians have established Bran Castle was built mostly for fortification and the protection of German colonists living in Transylvania.

This fortification began losing importance in 1836 when the borderline between Wallachia and Transylvania was moved, and the castle fell into disrepair. On Dec. 1, 1920 the castle was donated to Queen Marie of Romania who was determined to restore the castle, which then became her favorite residence.

So, if Vlad Țepeș never lived in Bran Castle and the infamous prince was the inspiration for the famed vampire in Stoker's novel, how did it become known as Dracula's Castle?

Simply put, Stoker got lucky. He never once mentions an exact location for the fictional construct, and he was never in Romania. He described Dracula's Castle as being at the confluence of three Romanian territories: Moldavia, Transylvania, and

See BRAN, page 44

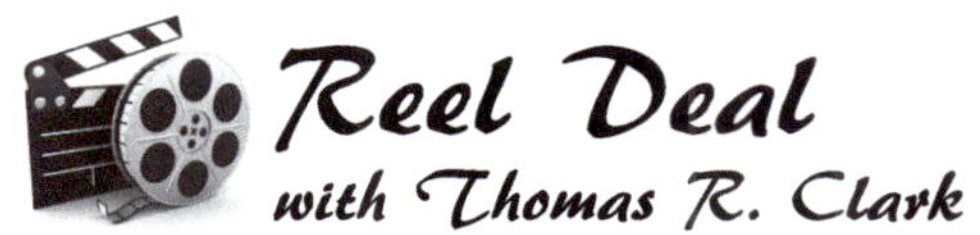

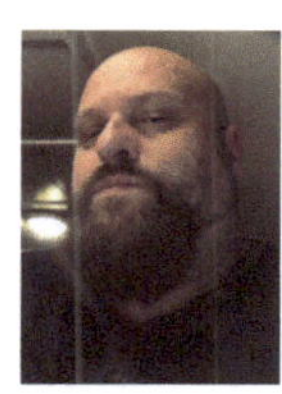

Carl Kolchak, the Greatest Writer Who Never Lived, or Why You Should Revisit the NIGHT STALKER

Man, 1974 was great. Yeah, I know it was 46 years ago, and it dates me, but I give no fucks. No cell phones, no internet or personal home computers, cable TV/HBO were new things. Life for a young man or woman in those days was filled with bell-bottoms, BMX, Evel Knievel, Bigfoot, and the radio or TV. Speaking of the latter, you only had maybe four channels. Yeah, you had to watch what was on when it was on because (gasp!) video recording was restricted to the rich at this point, but you know what? It didn't matter. Because network television in the 70s kicked fucking ass when it wanted to.

A pair of made-for-TV movies on ABC's Movie of the Week, which ran in 1972 and 1973, *The Night Stalker* and *The Night Strangler*, respectively, gained enough Neilsen ratings power the ABC execs thought they could pull off a weekly episodic, hourly drama. *The Night Stalker*'s 33.2 rating and 48 share meant most of America watched the movie. In modern terms, we're talking *Bird Box* on Netflix streaming numbers here, but in 1972!

So studio execs stopped production on a third Matheson scripted film, to be called *The Night Killers*, and put the allotted budget into what they believed would be a surefire hit. They thought wrong. The series adaptation imploded in one season, and the plug was pulled before all twenty-six planned episodes were produced.

The 1972 film and its 1973 sequel were written by Richard Matheson, the former from the novel *The Kolchak Tapes* by Jeff Rice, but Matheson didn't stick around for the TV series. Why did the two movies work, but not the series? All the other pieces were there, with Darren McGavin's frumpy and almost comical investigative reporter Carl Kolchak's charisma driving the bus. The movies played out like a police procedural, but with a reporter as the main focus, not a policeman. And man was this show scary. Wow! Not to mention the comic chemistry between McGavin and his foil, Simon Oakland's editor-in-chief Tony Vincenzo. All of it was there.

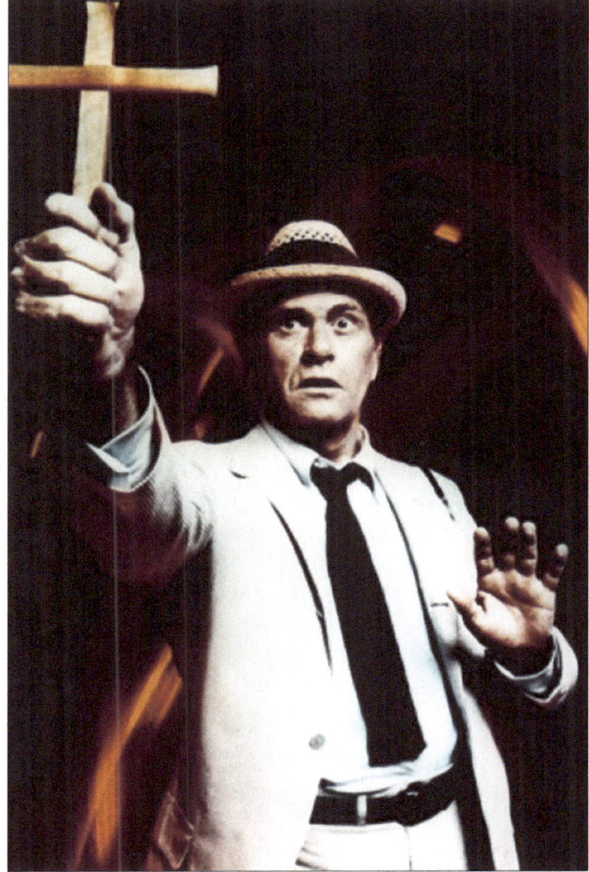

When the series aired, it failed to connect with viewers and became a dismal, Nielsen ratings nightmare. Its Friday night "death slot" at 10 p.m. didn't help. The show missed Matheson's writing, much of which now fell into the hands of star McGavin. Moving the setting to Chicago removed much of the exotic luster the movies had with their settings in Las Vegas and Seattle. A six month hiatus, including two more schedule changes and a name change to *Kolchak: The Night Stalker* … and the show was dead.

The Night Stalker didn't go away quietly into the night. Instead, it fought for life like the monsters depicted on the show and quickly became a cult classic. In a move of brilliant irony, by the early 80s, on any given Friday late-night on the CBS network, you could see reruns, incorporating the original films, and all ten episodes of the series, all summer long. Young people in that era loved Friday late-night CBS for this. I know. I was one of them.

The Night Stalker's legacy has been seen on television and the big screen for decades. Its "Monster of the week" format—though at the time shown disdain by its star, McGavin—has since gone on to be the template for many programs to follow. The X-Files, most specifically. This show went as far as to invite Darren McGavin on as a thank you. There's also *Grimm*, *Stranger Things*, and every ghost hunting show on cable or streaming service. They all share this movie and series as their biological grandfather.

Do yourself a favor and time travel with me back to the early 70s and revisit *The Night Stalker* series and TV movies. They're a quick weekend binge. I won't say all the episodes have aged well, but most of them, like its peer *The Twilight Zone*, still pack a powerful, thrill ride of a punch. Now under the aegis of NBC The *Night Stalker* has found a home at its third network in as many generations. (https://www.nbc.com/kolchak-the-night-stalker/) episodes You can stream all the episodes from NBC's app! I regret you won't find the two original films there. You can find *The Night Stalker* and *The Night Strangler* on YouTube, though.

In a Virtual World with Peter Molnar

Resident Evil 3 delivers as amped up 2020 reboot

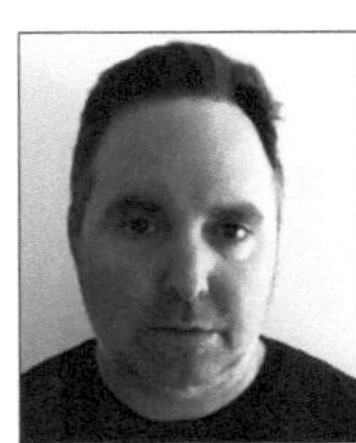

If somebody told me I would be playing through a reboot of *Resident Evil 3*—a game that centers around a horrific pandemic in which people in a metropolitan city contract a virus that turns them into zombies—while I was living in the midst of a real life pandemic of epic proportions, I may not necessarily have told them they were crazy. But I most certainly would have questioned how likely such a prediction could be. After all, in the last decade or so, the world has seen such viruses as Ebola and H1N1 come and go, having left numerous casualties in their wake. Such a thing as a pandemic has not existed outside the realm of possibility in quite some time. I am quite sure the irony is not lost on the game's developer, Capcom, either. However, I imagine they can draw some solace in the fact they have released a game for a time and place that will lend players some helpful distraction from their lives, which have been turned upside down in compliance with a slew of strange, new safety precautions.

This is exactly what *Resident Evil 3* offers its players. A welcome respite of fun and immersion.

For me, the best part about starting a new *Resident Evil* game is that moment right before it loads for the first time when one's fear of the unknown takes hold. I had already seen the screen captures, watched the advanced video reviews, and I had even played the original from twenty years ago. Still, I anticipated something frightening and exhilarating waiting to pounce the moment the game started. I had had a similar feeling preceding my first playthrough of *RE 7: Biohazard*. It had already been tagged as quite possibly the most frightening survival-horror RPG ever. I could only imagine what awaited me in that game. *RE 3* (Reboot) would be no exception, I figured. Then, the game started, with its incredibly moving and realistic news clips chronicling the world's rapid descent into crisis mode in the wake of the T-Virus pandemic. I watched in awe as the newly renovated Raccoon City burned and new zombies staggered across the screen after their sitting-duck victims, and I knew full well I was in for an adventure of monumental proportions. I was stoked Capcom had gotten it right ... again!

In 2019, Capcom "got it right" in a major way with the first reboot in the series for *Resident Evil 2*. It garnered universal critical acclaim as being one of the best reboots of all time and continues to wow latecomers. *Resident Evil 3* hits nearly all the right notes as *RE 2*. As *RE 2* takes places almost exclusively within the Raccoon City Police Department with its secret passageways and varied building levels, *RE 3* situates its main protagonist, Jill Valentine, in the center of the chaos of Racoon City proper. For a city in collapse, it has never looked better, from its shadowy alleyways to its cordoned off streets blocked by defunct buses and emergency vehicles, all delivered at a staggering 109 frames per second. Anyone who is new to the franchise need not worry as the corporation responsible for manufacturing the T-virus, Umbrella Corporation, is documented from its beginnings to its rise and eventual infamy. You can jump right into the action with a working knowledge of the backstory.

Action?

The new *RE3* grounds itself in the same level of fast paced, breakneck speed as the original. The structure of the game barely allows for you to take a breath before a handful of zombies are clawing at your throat or tearing a piece of it away. Not to mention, well, the most ever present, lurking, and terrifying threat embodied by Nemesis. Yes, Nemesis is a carryover from the original, but this "10-foot weaponized monster" resembles its former self in appearance only. In fact, the Nemesis of the first *RE3* was docile in comparison to the unstoppable behemoth who stalks Jill Valentine from the very beginning of the new *RE3*. Nemesis was designed and built by the Umbrella Corporation with one purpose only: to eliminate Jill Valentine. Nemesis harkens back to the Terminator of the silver screen, sent back in time to kill the leader of the Resistance, John Connor. And just like the Terminator, Nemesis can be staggered for mere moments. This provides Jill just enough time to utilize the new "Dodge" feature when seconds count. If you time this feature exactly right, time slows down, and you have a chance to fire off some rounds at Nemesis or any other nearby threats. For those who have played the *Resident Evil 2* reboot, Mr. X was the persistent, intimidating threat who relentlessly stalked you through the Raccoon Police Department. Equally unstoppable, but not nearly as mobile and threatening as Nemesis, who can snag you up with his whip-like tendrils or burst through a wall right beside you. Of course, when you do manage to escape Nemesis, the relief you feel is immediate and powerful.

The downside of the game is its scaling back of puzzles, which were abundant in both *RE2* and the original *RE3*. There are some, and you also must revisit and explore areas of the city over and over once you've obtained the right key to open storage containers or a tool that will make a fire hydrant useable or augment a particular weapon in your arsenal. And while there are not

See EVIL, page 47

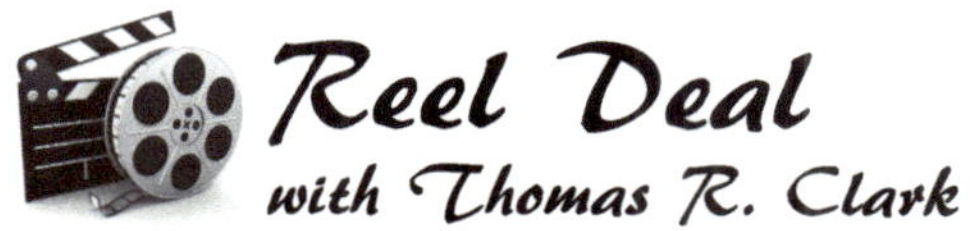

I COME TO SUCK YOUR ... FUN

How *What We Do in the Shadows* has saved the vampire horror genre

Vampires.

They're immortal, blood-sucking monsters, lurking in the darkness. And they've gone through more PR changes in the last 100ish years since Bram Stoker wrote Dracula than any other monster in fiction. Much of this is superfluous. Does sunlight kill them or does it make them shiny? Do they have fangs or not? Are they sexy romantic leads or are they desiccated corpses? Are they scary or are they funny? Are they metaphor for disease or negative human interactions? The combinations and outcomes are endless.

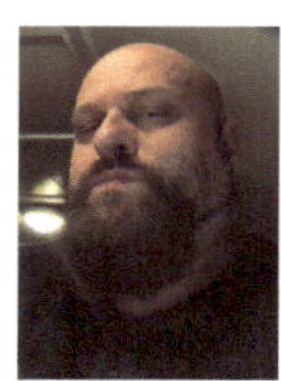

Because of this monster's resilience, it has fallen victim on more than one occasion to its own trope. Quite often, the previous generation's monsters become the focal point of parody by the next. This was seen starting with Universal's monsters, as they were often paired up with the comedy team of Bud Abbot and Lou Costello. As a result, an interesting domino effect comes into play. As generations pass, these monsters tend to become characters in children's entertainment.

Does *Monster Squad* ring any bells? Or how about *Transylvania 6500* or *Hotel Transylvania* as further examples? Fucking Dracula and the host of Universal's supernatural baddies in a kids' cartoons. It doesn't get worse than this unless you take into account bumblefest comedian Leslie Neilsen's *Dracula Dead and Loving it* or George Hamilton's awful *Love At First Bite*. In much the same manner as the campy *Batman* television show of the '60s put a serious hurting on Batman until Tim Burton brought the darkness, comedy vampires softened the public for the next blow to come.

The romantic, dayglow vampires of Stephanie Meyer's *Twilight* franchise put a stake through the vampire trope's heart with any serious vampire horror lover for nearly a decade. It seemed as though the vampires became a victim of their own longevity. No matter what masters do to save the genre, take Richard Matheson's *I Am Legend* into account, after a brief resurgence, it always seems to get dragged away in the tide.

This not to say there haven't been more saving grace gems along the way. *The Lost Boys*, *Near Dark*, and *Fright Night* secured the '80s. Coppola's *Bram Stoker's Dracula* led to the adaptation of Anne Rice's *Interview With the Vampire*. From *Dusk Til Dawn*, the *Underworld* series of films, and the television presence of sexy vampires playing off *Twilight* in *True Blood* and *The Vampire Diaries* all kept the trope in the public eye.

And now we've reached that time where comedy has been injected back into the vampire trope. There's only one difference between now and the previous comedy romps for our bloodsucking fiends. The current incarnation is both funny and scary and a perfect culmination of all that's come before it.

What We Do in the Shadows, a mockumentary from the mind of director wunderkind Taika Waititi (*Jojo Rabbit*) and Jermaine Clement, has turned the trope on its head. He took a group of vampires, added the element of a television production company, and created what can only be called *"The Office* with vampires." The success of the film led to the creation of the FX television

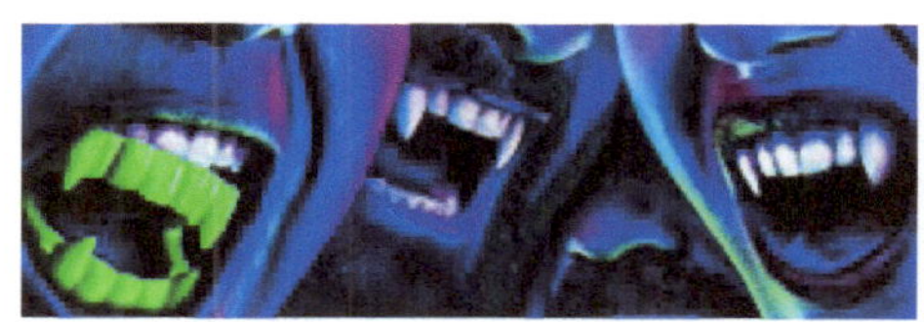

program which recently wrapped up its sophomore season. Like *M*A*S*H*, the TV show is better than the movie. Unlike *M*A*S*H*, it recognizes the previous motion picture incarnation.

And it's single handily saving the vampire trope.

Moving the action from New Zealand to Staten Island, New York, the stellar cast includes UK nerd genre vet Matt Berry (*The IT Crowd*) as Lazlo and newcomer Natasia Demetrio as his vampire wife Nadja. Their banter is classic husband and wife material that often falls into the perverse. Kayvan Novak plays 750-year-old former Iranian warlord, Nandor, and Harvey Guillen, whose character is an obvious homage to vampire horror master Guillermo del Toro, plays Nandor's (Novak) human familiar. He's so much an homage to del Toro, his fucking name is Guillermo. But it's Mark Proksch who steals the scenery as psychic vampire Colin Robinson.

A side character at most in the first season, Colin has evolved into *What We Do in the Shadows* Fonzie. He steps up to the plate for an appropriate "Ayyyyy!" when needed, drilling home dry and sarcastic humor Jerry Seinfeld wished he could muster. The thing about Colin is we all know him from our workplace or our own circle of friends. Yet for as brilliant as this character is, he's only one portion of the ingredients making this program, already renewed for a third season, work with all cylinders firing.

There is so much to laugh at. One side plot of Guillermo's ties to the Van Helsing family. The casual manner in which this apparently unathletic man is able to dispatch vampires will cause instant bursts of laughter. Guillermo desperately wants Nandor to turn him into a vampire, but instead, all the vampires do is disrespect him. Then there's Lazlo's hedge garden, an orgy of phallic and vaginal plant sculptures. Or his alter ego of Jackie Daytona, perfectly normal human bartender. How about Nadja's doll, introduced in season two, which is possessed by Nadja's own ghost, of course—I mean who else would it be? She gives such great advice.

The guest stars come from show creator and producer Waititi's associations in Hollywood. Which means Marvel/Disney. Guest spots from the likes of Doug Jones, Dave Baustista, Tilda Swinton, Evan Rachel Wood, Haley Joel Osment, and Danny Trejo. Shit, even Mark fucking Hamill and Pee-Wee Herman himself, Paul Reubens. Did I mention Wesley Snipes as ... Wesley the Daywalker?

The production design makes the show "real." *What We Do In The Shadows* is the natural evolution of classic TV

BRAN, cont. from page 43

Bukovina. The novel offers other tidbits to cement the inspiring castle in readers' minds, such as: "The driver was in the act of pulling up the horses in the courtyard of a vast ruined castle … The castle is on the very edge of a terrific precipice." In Stoker's time, Bran Castle checked all the boxes.

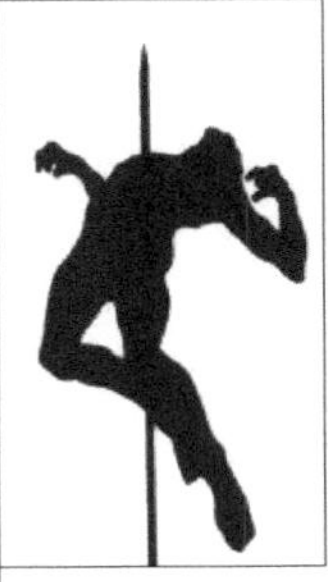

According to Bran residents today, at some point travelers to the region happened upon the castle in the mountains above the town and decided it must be the castle from Stoker's vampiric tome. Word spread from there.

For years the townspeople fought the designation, explaining in vain to tourists that Vlad Țepeș never lived in the castle let alone the area. But at some point, a town leader realized a benefit to going along with it, and if people wanted to believe it is Castle Dracula, then so be it. They could at least benefit from the tourism this belief brought.

However, according to Life magazine's 2016 issue titled "The World's Most Haunted Places," many Romanians resent the characterization of their country as a haunted land filled with mystery, superstition, and doom. Trent Leinenbach, a Brigham Young University student at the time, is quoted as saying Romanians are aware of the country's spooky reputation but the people he encountered don't seem interested in that side of the folklore.

But many of the older Transylvanians are said to continue to believe in ghosts, vampires, werewolves, witches, and forest spirits. According to the short Life article, these legends are unfortunately dying out, which is reportedly why Britain's Prince Charles (believed to be a descendent of Vlad Țepeș) started a foundation to preserve Romanian heritage.

"I do have a bit of a stake in the country," the prince said. "Transylvania is in my blood."

Regardless of whether you believe Bran Castle is the inspiration for Castle Dracula, it is worth a visit should you have opportunity to go. The villages still maintain a quaint atmosphere, the countryside is beautiful and striking, and even a sunny day can hold a bit of an eerie vibe.

EVIL, cont. from page 45

many puzzles in the *RE3* reboot, those few are quite challenging. Solving the puzzles in the reboot is deeply satisfying and serves the story in a meaningful way.

I also found it somewhat frustrating a game that touts itself as "open world" does not live up to such a moniker. When I think of open world gameplay design, there is no nook or cranny of the environment I cannot explore or inhabit as needed. *RE3* keeps you locked onto the path of the story but provides the illusion that you have more choice in the matter than you actually do. With environments so vividly constructed, I found myself wanting to wander off the beaten path of the story and could not. This was an early frustration, and the immersive story and satisfaction in popping off zombie heads with your sidearm over and over made up for this shortcoming quickly.

The multiplayer aspect of the game, titled "Resistance", allows you to play as either Survivor or Mastermind. As a Survivor, you team up with others in a 4v1 mode to kills hosts of zombies and gather keys. Each Survivor possesses their own special skill, and it is up to you and your teammates to determine how best to use each other for maximum success in holding back the hordes and progressing through asymmetrical maps. Conversely, as Mastermind you work to terrorize and sabotage the Survivors by arranging elaborate traps to corral them for a zombie feast they cannot escape. It all depends what your pleasure is, good or evil. Sometimes it's fun to step outside the norm of the hero in a game and delve into your darker side. I enjoyed tapping into this dark side and controlling the fates of the Survivors. Whether you play a match as Survivor or Mastermind, the thrill is fantastic. And for me, *bad* never felt so good!

Resident Evil 3 (2020), like its *RE2* Reboot predecessor, stands as a virtual blueprint for what a reboot should be. It should exhibit significant improvement on all fronts, from design to gameplay to DLC. With the amping up of Nemesis' threat level, as well as the deeper storyline and heart pounding action from moment to moment, Capcom has another updating triumph on their hands. I can only imagine what their reimagining of *Resident Evil 4*, my favorite of the franchise, will look like. Hopefully, they will serve up yet another brilliant update!

Rating: 9/10

SHADOWS, cont. from page 45

shows like *The Addams Family* and *The Munsters*. But unlike them, for as funny as the show is, this is still a horror genre program. The vampires, when not being comical, are scary as fuck. *What We Do In The Shadows* has mastered the offscreen scare with what it doesn't' show you in the daily lives of these undead creatures. We are reminded Guillermo's job is to supply these fiends with food. And though we laugh at their antics for thirty minutes, we are often reminded there are 23 and a half more hours in a day when terrifying things happen in this house in Staten Island. It's this hidden horror that gives you a shiver between belly laughs.

What We Do In The Shadows is a bingeable series you'll want to revisit to catch the jokes you missed while you guffawed at some visual prank or play on words. The show easily could have gone south and done more damage to the vampire genre than good. Instead, it's revitalized a trope left out to die as the sun rises, giving it the strength to hide in the shadows and wait to strike at its next victim. Vampires are returning to screens again. Not all are hits, Netflix's adaptation of IDW's *V-Wars* failed for being an uninspired rehash of Del Toro's *The Strain*. But BBC's *Dracula* reimagination was a hit with viewers.

With *What We Do In The Shadows* at the forefront of a vampire genre resurgence, we'll soon be seeing another *Salem's Lot* remake, for example. AMC has paid Anne Rice a handsome retainer to produce her *Vampire Chronicles*, which would make it the fourth, high production horror genre program on the network. Are vampires and zombies strong enough to hold the network up? We'll see. Until then, I'm going to wait for season three of a brilliant, albeit often horrific, laugh fest.

www.ingramcontent.com/pod-product-compliance
Lightning Source LLC
LaVergne TN
LVHW070155110826
845147LV00002B/405

* 9 7 8 1 9 4 5 2 6 3 2 0 0 *